RIGHT HAND

RIGHT HAND

The Hero Who Lives Next Door

Farkenfield Trilogy Book III

Jim Gallman

This book is a work of fiction. Unless otherwise indicated, the names, characters, businesses, places, events, and incidents, are either the product of the author's imagination or used in a fictitious manner. Any resemblance to actual persons, living or dead, or actual events is purely coincidental and used to further the fictional narrative.

Heart disease is the leading cause of death among men and women but twice as many men die of cardiovascular diseases. Risk factors include:

    Diabetes
    Family history
    High blood pressure
    High cholesterol
    Physical inactivity
    Obesity/overweight
    Smoking

An ounce of prevention is worth a pound of cure. If you wait too long to make life changes you may be counted as one of the people who die from heart disease. The book *Forks Over Knives* by Dr. Colin Campbell is an informative read on disease prevention.

DEDICATION

To my 100-year-old mother, Martha Gallman,
Pat, my wife of 59 years, my sons Jay and John,
and Maggie, my miniature Schnauzer.

ACKNOWLEDGMENTS

I want to thank all the people who go about their lives anonymously making our world a better place to live. All superheroes don't wear capes or have superpowers. They are our neighbors, who teach our children, fill our prescriptions, work in our hospitals, serve in our military, drive the trucks that deliver our goods, work on farms, or in many other service jobs. The Covid pandemic showed us who the real superheroes are in our society.

Next, I want to thank my family and Maggie for giving me love and support.

My books would not be possible without the talent of *Virtual Office Assistance Professionals*.

Finally, thank you for reading my work. Your feedback is welcomed.

You can contact me at *BamaBoyPublishing@gmail.com*.

Jim Gallman

CONTENTS

INTRODUCTION

Three young boys, JB Farkenfield, George Daniel Franklin, and Robert Talbert, who from the first day of first grade would be called "Right Hand", met in Mrs. Burns' first grade class at Woodstock Elementary School. They became lifelong friends.

Growing up in the segregated South their lives were filled with football, hunting, fishing, girls, and church on Sunday. The Vietnam war, which disrupted the lives of many young men of their generation, took them down three different paths.

JB's path was chronicled in *Holes in the Sky, A Story of Retribution and Redemption.*
George Daniel Franklin's story was told in *DoomsDay Dan.*

This is Right Hand's story.

CHAPTER 1

The first Sunday in June 1976 the church I attended had a visiting speaker from Open Doors USA. Open Doors International was founded by a Dutch minister, Andrew van der Bijl, who was called Brother Andrew and was known as God's Smuggler. A fitting nickname since he smuggled Bibles into Communist countries where Christians were persecuted. At the conclusion of his speech, a special offering was held to pay for Bibles, and I wrote a check for $100.

Sunday night as I lay in bed, I could not get it out of my head that I had not done enough. It was too easy to write a check and think I had done my duty as a good Christian. I tossed and turned all night fighting with my conscience about what I should do. On Monday I made a phone call that would change my life.

In September, I told my friends I was going on a Christian mission to Finland. On the flight to New York, I questioned if I was truly ready to put my life on the line for my Christian beliefs. Was I a fool to leave my wife and family and go on a mission where I may be putting my family's welfare in jeopardy? During the hours from New York to Helsinki I thought about what had brought me to this point in my life. As a boy growing up, my mother and father often recounted stories of our family's history, which was steeped in Christian values, hard work, and loyalty.

In 1916, my grandfather Herbert got tired of trying to scratch a living out of the red clay of Cleburne County, Alabama. The small farm which he had inherited from his father barely kept him and grandma alive. They worked from daylight to dark and went to bed with their stomachs gnawing on their back bones many nights. Their clothes were rags, patches on top of patches. If it were not for his hound dog and gun, they would have starved to death.

As the frigid night winds howled in January 1916, he knew that he couldn't face another planting season where the weather and pests destroyed his corn crop. A friend at church told him he should move to Anniston where there were good paying jobs for anyone who was willing to work. His only other alternative was to become a moonshiner. Many small farmers had turned to making whiskey from their meager corn crops to survive, but being a Baptist, he was against alcohol.

After discussing it Sunday night, Grandpa and Grandma decided they had to make a change. Monday morning before daylight he and Grandma bundled up in their winter clothes, wrapped up in quilts and rode in the wagon the 20 miles into Anniston. They had left way before daybreak so they could get to the hiring office of Anniston Cotton Manufacturing Company, a large cotton mill, before it closed for the day. It had been built by two leading Anniston industrialists, Sam Noble and Alfred Tyler, as a companion industry to the city's growing iron industry as a source of employment for the wives and children of the iron workers. Just after one o'clock, they climbed down from the wagon and with butterflies in their stomachs, walked into the hiring office located at 215 West Eleventh Street.

"May I help you?" the receptionist asked.

"Yes ma'am, we would like to see about getting work here in the mill," my grandpa replied.

The receptionist reached into her desk drawer and pulled out some paperwork. "You will have to fill out job applications and the personnel manager will review them. If he has jobs to offer you, he will mail you a letter." She paused before handing Grandpa the paperwork, "Can you read and write, or do you want me to fill out the form for you?"

"We can both read and write. Would it be possible for the boss to review our applications today and tell us if we are going to get a job? We live on a farm in Cleburne County and must ride into Heflin to get mail."

When Grandpa handed back the completed applications, the receptionist gave them a quick once-over. "Have a seat and let me see if Mr. Morgan has time to interview you today." She rose and opened the door beside her desk and disappeared down a short hallway.

"You're in luck. Mr. Morgan can see you now. Please follow me."

"Come in Mr. and Mrs. Talbert. I'm Ernest Morgan. It's a pleasure to meet you both," he said as he offered his hand to Grandpa. "So, I see you have decided to give up farming and move to Anniston. Please have a seat. Let me tell you about the jobs I have available at this time. Mrs. Talbert, I have an opening in the spinning room tending the machines that spin the cotton into thread. That pays fifteen cents per hour. And, Mr. Talbert, being a farmer, I assume you're handy."

"Yes sir, I don't mean to brag, but I can fix most anything that needs fixing."

"Good, because I have a job in the maintenance department, oiling the machines and helping repair them when they break. Sounds like that's a job that suits you. It pays twenty cents per hour."

Grandma cast a quick glance at Grandpa wondering if they'd just hit the jackpot. Mr. Morgan continued speaking as if he'd recited the words hundreds of times.

"A big benefit our company offers is low rent in the mill village. You can rent a two-bedroom house with a kitchen, living room, and an indoor toilet for $2 a week. You can shop at the company general store and charge your purchases, and for a small fee, you can be seen by the company doctor in the company medical clinic. The rent and what you charge at the general store and doctor's fees will be deducted from your weekly pay. After paying rent and federal income tax y'all will have $14.46 a week to spend. We also provide a school for the children of our employees and a nursery for the small children of our female workers at no cost. And, of course, there is a church in the village you can attend if you wish. The company also has a baseball team and a recreation center. Do you have any questions?"

"No sir, that would seem to cover all the bases," Grandpa quipped. Mr. Morgan didn't get the pun.

It didn't take a minute for Grandpa and Grandma to decide to give up farming and move to the city. They signed their employment papers and for a house in the village. They were all smiles as they climbed up on the wagon to begin their last ride back to the farm. Sunday at church they announced they were moving to Anniston. They gave their chickens to the preacher and offered to sell their cow and pigs for a decent price to the family who lived a mile down the road. They loaded up their one-horse wagon with the few household possessions they owned and their hound dog, Blue, and moved to Anniston where they happily joined the ranks of the army of "lint heads" who worked in cotton mills throughout the South.

On Wednesday, Mavis and Herbert moved into the house at 601 Pine Avenue. To most people it was a very modest house but to my grandparents it was a mansion. Grandma could not believe that they had an indoor toilet and electric lights. Anniston had been the first town in Alabama to have electricity. Many parts of rural Alabama would not get electricity until in the early '50s. Grandma would stand and stare at the toilet every time she pulled the chain, watching it flush.

"Herbert, where do you think the water goes?" she asked. "Do you think it goes under the house? It will begin to smell before long."

Before Herbert could answer her there was a knock at the front door. A woman about their age stood on the porch, smiling. "Hello, I'm Mable Whitiger, your next-door neighbor. Welcome to the Village."

"Why thank you, Ms. Mable. Come on in out of the cold," Grandpa said as he held the door for her.

"I appreciate the invitation, and I'll take you up on your offer another time. I just got off work, or I would have been over earlier, and I need to tend to some things at home. Just wanted to let you know, if y'all need anything to get settled in, just come over and knock on my door."

Mable paused to take in our wagon and old horse. "You know, you can't keep your horse tied up in the yard. We sold our mule and cow to Mr. Thomas who lives at the base of Cold Water Mountain just off the Eastaboga Road. You can't miss it if you go west on Tenth Street."

That knock on the door was the beginning of a thirty-year friendship between Mavis and Mable.

The next morning Grandpa rode out to Mr. Thomas's farm and sold the horse and wagon. When summer came, Mr. Thomas came through the mill village selling fresh produce off the wagon that Grandpa had sold him.

Monday morning, they started work in the mill. Grandma was introduced to the other ladies working in the spinning room and got a thirty-minute instruction on her new job by the foreman. Grandpa was given an oil can and assigned to one of the machine mechanics.

While some people complained about working six days a week, Herbert and Mavis knew they had found the answer to their prayers. They were making more money in a week than they made in six months on the farm. From the sale of the livestock and the wagon, they had $20 in cash in the cookie jar for the first time since they were married.

Grandpa wasn't bragging when he told Mr. Morgan that he had a natural ability to fix machines. He told Grandma he could see the machine in his mind and knew what a machine sounded like when it was working properly. The maintenance foreman was amazed at how fast Grandpa learned the workings of all the machines. Six months after he started on the job he was promoted to machine mechanic and got a nickel an hour raise. If there was a problem that had a mechanic stumped, the foreman would call Grandpa to come diagnose the problem and tell them what needed to be fixed. Word soon spread through the mill that

Grandpa was a mechanical genius. Grandma said his brain was wired differently than most people.

In late March as the grass turned green, the Mill baseball team started practicing for the start of the six team, semi-pro East Alabama Cotton Mill Baseball League. The league was made up of Anniston Manufacturing, Oxford Cotton Mill, Blue Mountain Mills, Jacksonville Cotton Mill, Piedmont Mills and Talladega Bag. Grandpa had never played baseball, but a neighbor encouraged him to come watch a practice. The team had a pitcher who had a curveball that no one on the team could hit. Grandpa watched as the pitcher made fools of the hitters.

After watching for a little while, Grandpa could see the pitches in his mind. He knew just when the ball would break and when the hitter should swing to hit the ball. He asked the coach if he could have a try at hitting. Grandpa stepped into the batter's box and the pitcher threw a hard fast ball towards Grandpa's head. Grandpa moved out of the way of the pitch at the last second, noticing that the pitcher had a slight difference in his delivery when he threw a curveball.

The next pitch was the curveball. It looked like it was going to hit the batter but then it would curve over the plate for a strike. Grandpa swung the bat and made contact with the ball. It was a long fly ball that cleared the left field fence. The pitcher said it was a lucky hit, but Grandpa kept hitting the ball deep to the outfield and line drives and grounders. Every time the pitcher wound up Grandpa knew where the ball was going to go. Grandpa had memorized the pitcher's delivery and knew the slight differences in his pitches.

"Damn man, you are some hitter. What team have you played for?" the pitcher asked as they headed for the dugout.

"Never played the game in my life," Grandpa responded, "That was the first time I have ever held a bat in my hand."

"You know you'll go to hell for lying," the pitcher chided.

"No lie, it was the first time," Grandpa insisted.

Overhearing the conversation, the coach told Grandpa, "Grab a glove and get out to right field. I want to see you field some fly balls."

Grandpa got a glove and trotted out to right field. The coach hit a fly ball and Grandpa watched it land in front of him. He walked over and picked it up and threw it back to the coach on one pounce. The coach hit another fly ball. Grandpa's brain did the geometry and told him right where he needed to run to catch the ball. He then threw a strike to the catcher at home plate. The coach waved for him to come in.

"Enough of your 'I've never played before' bullshit. No one can hit like that and throw the ball from right field on a line to home plate who has never played baseball before."

Grandpa took offense, "I'm not a liar and I don't appreciate being called one."

"Sorry, but I've never seen anyone with so much natural ability to play the game," the coach offered contritely. "What's your name and what department do you work in?"

"Herbert Talbert and I work in maintenance."

"Well, Herbert, how would you like to be our starting right fielder? Starting players get a dollar a game. That's $20 for the regular season. We play our home games on Sunday afternoons at Zinn Park. If we win the league, we get to go to the Cotton Mill World Series Tournament at West Point, Georgia in September. The Mill pays for all travel and meals when we travel out of town."

Without hesitation, Grandpa said yes, and he was given a uniform, a glove, and a pair of spikes.

The first Sunday in April a large crowd of people showed up to Zinn Park for the game between Anniston Manufacturing and Blue Mountain Mills. The crowd who had ridden the trolley down from Blue Mountain were seated along the third base foul line. Grandma and Mable Whitiger had packed a picnic lunch and were sitting along the first base line with the crowd from Anniston Manufacturing. She was excited to see Grandpa play in his first game. The crowd on both sides were loud and some were well on the way to being drunk. Blue Mountain was the betting favorite to win the game because they had won the league championship last season.

Grandpa and the Anniston Manufacturing Spinners took the field to a loud roar. The pitcher's curveball worked its magic and Blue Mountain went down one, two, three. Grandpa caught a fly ball in right field for the third out. There was no score until the third inning when Grandpa, who was batting eighth, came up to bat for the first time.

Grandpa had been studying the pitcher and knew what he would pitch before he threw the ball. He always started off with a high fastball up around the letters followed by a sinker that dropped out of the strike zone. Grandpa didn't wait for the second pitch, he hit the high fast ball over the center field fence. Grandma almost choked on her sandwich as she jumped up and down and yelled along with the Spinners fans. The score held up until the top of the ninth inning, when Blue Mountain scored to tie the game.

Grandpa was the leadoff hitter in the bottom of the ninth. He walked on four pitches then stole second. A long fly ball got him over to third. The Spinners coach gave the sign for a suicide bunt. When the pitcher released the pitch Grandpa broke for home and the batter laid down a perfect bunt down the first base line. The pitcher fielded the bunt and threw the ball to the catcher, but Grandpa slid under the tag ending the game.

Grandpa was selected for the All-Star team that season, but Talladega Bag won the championship. After the end of the season, the coach of Blue Mountain sent a letter to Grandpa offering him a job at thirty cents an hour, a free house, and $3 a game. Grandpa took the letter to Mr. Morgan. The next day the General Manager called Grandpa into his office. He beat the Blue Mountain offer and told him he would be moved up to Assistant Foreman of the Maintenance Department when the Assistant Foreman retired in six months.

When Grandpa got home that evening he told Grandma, "Mavis, I've got some good news. I got another promotion. Now,

I'm making what we were both making, and we get free rent, so you don't have to work anymore."

"Well, Herbert, that is good news, because I would have to stop working before long anyway. I'm pregnant."

On April 3, 1917, Grandpa missed the opening game of the baseball season because my father was born. Grandpa and Grandma named him Samual Alfred after the men who had built Anniston Manufacturing. The next year, on July 12, 1918, my Aunt Sandra was born, but she was considerate enough to be born on a Tuesday, so Grandpa didn't miss a game.

CHAPTER 2

I spent the first four hours of my flight to Finland second-guessing the choices I made that put me on this path. My thoughts were all over the map, but my biggest worry was how my decision would affect my family. They were no strangers to difficulty and the curve-balls life could throw at you. My dad certainly had a few.

Dad graduated from Alabama Polytechnic Institute in June of 1939 with a degree in Textile Engineering, and that summer while playing for the Cotton Mill All Stars Dad hurt his knee sliding into second base. That ended his baseball playing and would have a profound effect on his life in the next few years.

In September, Dad walked into the Carnegie Library with the intention of checking out a copy of *The Grapes of Wrath* by John Steinbeck, the number-one bestseller that year. He walked up to the checkout desk and lost his heart. The librarian was so beautiful she took his breath away.

"How can I help you?" she asked.

"Marry me, Ellen." Dad replied with his winning smile, reading her name tag.

Ignoring the come-on, she asked, "Do you want to check-out the book in your hand?"

"Ah, yes I do," Dad replied.

"May I have your library card please?"

When he handed it over, their fingers touched, and he saw a flicker of recognition in Ellen's eyes that she didn't mind the contact.

"Mr. Talbert, the book is due back in two weeks. There is a two-cent fine each day it's late."

Two weeks later my dad was back in the library.

"Mr. Talbert, you don't have to check-in your book at the desk. You can drop it in the book return slot."

"Yes, I could have, but then I wouldn't get to talk to you."

Ellen blushed and smiled, revealing dimples on her cheeks. "Do you need a recommendation on another book to read?"

"No, but I'd like to know, would you go out with me?"

Ignoring his question, she replied, "Mr. Talbert, If you don't want to check out a book there are people waiting in line."

My dad walked back to the shelf for the best sellers and grabbed *The Citadel* by A.J. Cronin and got back in the line at the check-out desk. When he got up to the desk, there was no one behind him.

He handed over his library card and to his surprise, Ellen said, "If you come back at 5:30 when the library closes, you may walk me home."

"Ellen, that would be my pleasure. I'll be here."

At twenty-five minutes past five Dad walked into the library and up to the reception desk.

"Hello Mr. Talbert. I'm just finishing up and I'll be ready in a few minutes. I do so appreciate a man who's punctual."

"I aim to please, Ellen. Would you mind calling me Sam? And do you mind if we take my car?"

"Oh, Sam, I would rather walk. I live on East Twelfth so we would have time to get to know each other better."

Every day for the next week Dad was at the library at 5:30 and walked Emily home. After saying good-bye at her door Dad had to walk back to the library to get his car. After the third day, he told grandma that he had met the one he was going to marry.

After the fourth day of walking Ellen home after work, my dad got up the nerve to hold her hand as they walked. When they got to the door of her apartment he asked, "Have you seen the new movie, 'The Wizard of Oz'? It's playing at the Ritz."

"No, I haven't."

"Would you like to go Saturday night?"

"I would enjoy that very much, Sam."

"It starts at 7 so I'll pick you up at 6:30."

"That would be fine, Sam, but please don't park your car in front of my apartment. My neighbor is a busybody and likes to talk about all the neighbors. Could you park at least a block away and we can walk to the theater? It's not that far and I love to walk."

Her request was a little strange but if she had asked him to arrive in an ox cart, he would have said okay.

Saturday night Dad parked his car two blocks away and walked to Ellen's apartment. When they got to the theater there was a long line to buy tickets.

"Sam, how about we go have coffee and talk rather than go to the movies? There's a small bakery just down the street that has great pastries and good coffee."

A bit disappointed that he'd miss sitting close to Ellen in a darkened theatre, Dad agreed. They sat in a booth and talked as they ate their donuts and drank their coffee. He learned that Ellen was from Pennsylvania and her father had been stationed at Fort McClellan. She graduated in 1938 from Jacksonville State Teachers College with a major in Library Science and landed the job at the Carnegie Library.

Eventually, when I was old enough, Dad filled in the rest of his story about Ellen. After an hour or so at the bakery, Ellen suggested they go back to her apartment and listen to the latest Glenn Miller record she had just bought. Dad was so mesmerized by her he would have followed her to the city dump to eat garbage if she had asked him. When they got to her apartment, she moved the coffee table and rolled back the rug and they danced to Glenn Miller. She laid her head on Dad's shoulder and nibbled on his neck.

As the third song ended, she told Dad she was going to change into something more comfortable. When she came out of her bedroom she was wearing a big smile, and nothing else. She wiggled her finger in the "come here" gesture and Dad followed her into the bedroom. This librarian knew a lot more than just how to file books according to the Dewey Decimal System.

Just before midnight, she told him she had to get up early for church so he would have to leave. Dad got up, put on his clothes, and asked her if he could see her Sunday after church.

"I'm sorry but I always spend Sunday afternoon with my mother, but you can walk me home after work Monday afternoon."

Monday afternoon after work, they walked up to the Sanitary Cafe on Noble Street and had dinner. As they were walking past Collins Drug Store, she suggested that he should buy some protection just in case they decided to dance again. She walked down the street window-shopping, while, for the first time, Dad bought prophylactics from a drug store rather than from a machine in a filling station bathroom. They danced every night for the next week. When Dad asked her if she would like to go to the movies because "The Wizard of Oz" was only playing for five more days, she just smiled and said, "I would rather dance with you Sam."

This went on for about a month. One day at work a guy from the Accounting Department came up to him and said he needed to talk to Dad in private. They walked to the end of the hall and stepped into the stairway.

"I saw you in the Sanitary Cafe the other night with the woman from the library. She goes to my church. I don't want to get into your business, but do you know she is married to a soldier from the Fort who was sent to Panama about six months ago?"

Hiding his surprise, my dad searched for a response that would deflect suspicion. "No, I didn't know she was married. The subject didn't come up. We were having a conversation about a book she recommended and talking about John Steinbeck. Have you read *Grapes of Wrath?*"

For the remainder of the day Dad couldn't get the fact that Ellen had deceived him out of his mind, and he stopped going to the library. A week later his secretary told him, "The library called and said you have a book past due and asked that you please return it today. It must be a popular book for them to call and remind you to return it."

Dad ignored the message and didn't go back to the library for two weeks but his desire to read *The Snows of Kilimanjaro* by Ernest Hemingway overcame his reluctance to see Ellen again. As he walked up to the check-out desk with the book, there she was with her beautiful smile and long blonde hair.

He said nothing as he handed her his library card. "Long time, no see. Why didn't you come by?" she asked.

Her smile was radiant, and she was obviously happy to see him again. His thoughts vacillated between memories of their nights spent together to the disappoint, even anger, at her deception. "Ellen, one of my co-workers saw us having coffee at the Sanitary Café. He's also a member of your church."

He could tell she knew what was coming as she dropped her eyes. "Ellen, why didn't you tell me you were married? I don't go out with married women."

She lowered her voice and looked him in the eye, "Sam, for the past few months, I've been in the process of getting a divorce. I'm now a single woman."

He felt a glimmer of hope blossom. "You should have told me in the beginning, Ellen. Relationships are built on honesty and trust."

That smile, her ruby red lips, long blonde hair, and her dancing ability led my dad back to the apartment on East Twelfth Street. He read more books that winter than he had ever read before. Any excuse to go to the library. In March of 1940, Ellen told Dad she was moving to Atlanta, and going back to school to get a degree in law. She would become the first woman judge in the state of Georgia and one of only a few in the United States.

After she moved, Dad very seldom went to the library. He did drive over to Atlanta a couple of times, but the last time she told him that she was seeing someone else, and their dancing days were over.

Recalling Dad's story and the lesson that relationships are built on trust and honesty, my conscious was heavy. I had not honored his example with my own family and been honest about the mission I had embarked upon.

CHAPTER 3

Boredom overtook me around the fifth hour of my flight. My neighbor had the window seat and had fallen asleep as soon as we were airborne. I couldn't sleep, so I started reading the sports page of the newspaper I bought before boarding.

"How are the Braves doing?" my neighbor, who was now awake, asked. "Ted Turner should stick to television and leave sports to fellas that know what they're doing."

I nodded agreement and kept reading.

"Name's Art Nathanson," my neighbor said, offering his hand.

I shook it. "Robert Talbert, but everyone calls me Right Hand. Nice to meet you."

I had worn my dad's old ball cap which was tucked into the pouch in front of my seat.

"Hey, you're from Anniston?" Art asked, pointing to the hat emblazoned with Anniston Manufacturing Spinners. "That cap looks like it's seen some history."

I folded up my paper, realizing my talkative neighbor wasn't going to let me read. "Yep, that cap's seen a few games," I offered, smiling at the memories.

"Did you play?" Art asked.

"Not for long. Tore up my knee before I really got started, but I come a long line of ball players."

"Anybody I'd know?"

"No, but my dad got hits off Satchel Paige."

"No way, you're pulling my leg."

"It's a fact." I settled in and began a trip down memory lane.

The summer my father turned thirteen he spent the time playing baseball, fishing, and running the ridges. By the time Dad got to high school, he was just over six-feet-tall and muscular like my grandfather. Dad was one of the best baseball players on the sand lots of Anniston. Like Grandpa, he had a natural ability for the game. He was the starting shortstop for Anniston High School for three years and in the summers he played shortstop for the Spinners.

My dad graduated from Anniston High School on June 2, 1935. The whole family was in the auditorium when Dad walked across the stage and received his diploma. The next day he was at work in the mill making money to pay for his first year at the Alabama Polytechnic Institute. That summer the Spinners won the East Alabama Cotton Mill League championship and were invited to play in the first National Baseball Congress Semi-Pro Tournament World Series in Wichita, Kansas held August 13–27. The mill paid for the team to travel to Wichita, Kansas by train. Most of the players had never been further from Anniston than West Point, Georgia and had never ridden on a train.

There was a large crowd at the train station to see the team off. A reporter from the *Anniston Star*, the local newspaper, traveled with the team to report back the results of the games. The Spinners won their first game 12–6 and the *Anniston Star* had the story at the top of the sports page on the 14th. They lost in the second round to the Bismarck Churchills of North Dakota.

The players from Anniston had never played against an integrated team before. The Churchills' roster was made up of white minor leaguers and players from the Negro leagues. Their starting pitcher, Satchel Paige, was the star player from the Negro leagues and got paid $1,000 to play. Negro players could not play in the major leagues in 1935. He won four games and struck out 60 batters on the way to being named the MVP of the tournament. At the age of 42, he would go on to play in the major leagues in 1948, a year after Jackie Robinson broke the color barrier. The day after the Spinners lost, the *Anniston Star* sports page headline read "Spinners Lose to Integrated Team". My dad and my grandpa would brag for years that they had gotten hits off the famous Satchel Paige.

The summer of 1936 Grandpa coached a team called the Cotton Mill All Stars, made up of the best players from all six teams in the East Alabama Cotton Mill League. They took on all comers from throughout the South. They only lost one game 5–4 to the Bona Allen Shoemakers from Buford, Georgia. The two teams met again in the National Baseball Congress Tournament. The Cotton Mill All Stars lost the game 1–0 in ten innings. The Shoemakers lost to Haliburton of Oklahoma 4–1 in the championship game. They would come in second again in 1937 but the third time was the charm for the Shoemakers; they would win the championship in 1938.

"Wow, that's quite a story. I've been living in the South for a couple of years and had no idea about the history of the old leagues," Art offered, suitably impressed with my story-telling ability.

We were at the half-way point in our travel and the stewardesses were serving food and drinks. While I tucked into my meal my mind kept travelling back to the stories the family would recount sitting around our dinner table.

It was 1940 and the United States was coming out of the Great Depression and Germany was trying to take over all of Europe. The cotton mills were running full time, and the foundries were expanding their work forces. On Tuesday August 27th, the day FDR nationalized the National Guard in anticipation the U.S. would soon be joining the war in Europe, the phone rang in Dad's office.

"Hey Samuel, what are you doing Saturday night?"

"Who is this?" Dad asked, pretending he didn't recognize the voice.

"Who is this? It's your favorite banker. You know who this is," his friend Ben Sanders replied.

Dad chuckled, "Dad and I are going to the Anniston Rams baseball game. Why do you ask?"

"Well, you know I'm dating Betty Summers. Betty and her roommate from Montevallo Women's College are going to be in town this weekend and I need someone for her roommate to date or I don't get to go out with Betty. Do me a favor and be her date. I'll owe you big time."

"Where are you going?" Dad asked.

"We're going to a dance at Oxford Lake. They're having a ten-piece band from Atlanta that sounds just like Glenn Miller."

Since his dalliance with the librarian, my dad hadn't dated anyone. He was concentrating on his job and trying to get the librarian out of his head. Now, visions of Ellen and Glenn Miller on the record player danced in my head.

"Sorry, Ben. I already promised Dad we'd go to the ballgame."

"Damn it Samuel, you can go to the Sunday ballgame with your dad."

"Sorry, I can't"

"I'll pay for the tickets. Do me this favor and I'll owe you two favors," Ben begged.

Dad knew my grandpa didn't care if they saw the game on Saturday or Sunday, but he was enjoying hearing the desperation in Ben' voice. Ben was my dad's old roommate from college and had been his best friend from high school.

"Okay, but if the roommate is a dud, you'll owe me five favors." Dad teased.

"You won't regret it. I'll pick you up at six. See you Saturday. Make sure you have the cotton lint out of your hair."

Ben had gone to work in his father's bank when he graduated from college, and he was considered a very eligible bachelor by mothers with daughters they wanted to marry off.

Mrs. Summers was one of those mothers and she had worked diligently to get her daughter, Betty, matched up with Ben, the oldest son of the Sanders banking family, one of the wealthiest families in Anniston. Whoever caught Ben would move up in Anniston society. My dad was deemed less desirable by the matchmaking mothers because of his affair with the librarian and the fact our family were cotton-mill people. Most people in

Anniston didn't realize that by that time the Talbert family owned most of the land east of Hillside Cemetery. Grandpa had been buying up land since the roaring '20s.

Ben picked Dad up Saturday night and they drove over to Betty's house. Her father met them at the door and told them he expected them to have the girls home by eleven. When Betty's roommate walked down the stairs, Dad realized *he* owed Ben five favors. Ben would be a groomsman in my parent's wedding the next June.

Mom had short black hair, brown eyes, and an athletic build. She was on the Montevallo tennis team. As they got acquainted, Dad was impressed with her confident demeanor and her ability to discuss world events, to say nothing about her looks.

Oxford Lake was crowded with people. The music floated out of the dance hall and filled the amusement park that was next to the lake. It almost drowned out the yells from the people riding the Tilt-a-Whirl. The bright lights on the carousel and the Ferris wheel gave the park a festive appearance.

Although Calhoun County was a dry county, most of the people at the dance brought a flask or a pint bottle of whiskey to add to their cokes. Ben had a flask filled with rum because Betty loved rum and coke. She said it reduced her inhibitions so she could dance better. After three rum and cokes, she and Ben were dancing in the back seat of his car out in the dark parking lot.

During the band's intermission, Mom asked Dad if he would like to ride the Ferris wheel. The wheel stopped with them at the top so they could look out over the lake. Mom said it felt like they could reach up and touch the full moon. That is where my mom and dad had their first kiss.

Mom was from Birmingham, so just about every weekend Dad was driving the 64 miles to Birmingham to see Mom. If Mom couldn't come home on the weekend, Dad would drive the 96 miles to Montevallo. While driving back to Anniston late one Saturday night in January, after spending the day with Mom in Montevallo, a deer ran in front of Dad's car and he swerved to miss it, ran off the road and took out several small pine trees before the car came to a stop. Dad wasn't hurt but his 1932 Ford coupe had taken a beating. He was able to get the car started and get back on the highway and limp home.

He always called Mom when he got home because she said she worried about him driving at night. After he related his experience dodging the deer, she told him that in the future he would have to leave so he could get home before dark. Monday morning, he took his car to King Motors to have the dents fixed and to get a new paint job. Mr. King talked him into trading in his car for a 1940 Ford two-door sedan they had repossessed. It only had 3,000 miles on it and still had the new car smell. It had belonged to a man in the National Guard who couldn't afford to make the payments since FDR nationalized his unit and he had been sent to Camp Blanding in Florida.

On Valentine's Day 1941, Dad asked Mom to marry him, and she obviously said yes. But there was one problem that had to be solved before they could marry. Mom was Catholic and Dad had been raised Baptist. Her parents insisted the wedding be held at Saint Paul's Catholic Church in Birmingham and they wanted Dad to convert. If Mom had gone along with her parents that might have been a deal breaker, but they said they would compromise.

Mom and Dad would get married in the Catholic church and after they were married Mom would attend the Catholic church and Dad would go to the Baptist.

On June 2, 1941, Mom graduated from Montevallo Women's college with a degree in physical education.

At 5 PM, June 6, 1941, Mom got out of a Cadillac limousine and walked up the steps of Saint Paul's Catholic Church. She was 30 minutes late getting there. Over 200 people sitting inside, and my father, were beginning to think that Dad had been left at the altar. When Mom got to the front door of the church, her father met her and asked if she had changed her mind about going through with the marriage.

"It would not upset your mother and me if you decided not to marry out of your faith," her father said.

"No, Dad. I'm getting married. I'll explain why I'm late at the reception."

The wedding march began, and Mom's father escorted her as the guests stood and watched Mom glide down the aisle towards the anxious groom. Dad said he felt like his heart was beating so loud you could hear it all over the church. When he took Mom's hand and the priest said, "We are gathered here," he said his heart went back to its normal rhythm. Everything was a fog until Dad heard, "You may kiss your bride."

As they walked down the aisle as man and wife, Dad whispered to Mom, "Why were you so late?"

"I was getting you a surprise wedding gift," she replied.

At the wedding reception, Mom explained that on the way to the church a puppy had run out in front of the limousine nearly being run over. Concerned, she had the driver stop so she could catch the puppy to keep it from running out in the road again.

"You should have seen me chasing after a puppy in my wedding dress," she recounted as the guests laughed.

Mom and Dad named the puppy Lucky.

Grandpa gave Mom and Dad a lot on East Tenth Street for their wedding present. Mom and Dad rented a small apartment while their new house on East Tenth was being built. Mom got a job as the girls PE coach at Anniston High School. The part of the job she loved the most was coaching the boy's and girl's tennis teams. Much to the chagrin of their parents, Mom and Dad ended up joining the Methodist Church.

Life was good until December 7, 1942, the day that FDR said would live in infamy, when Japan bombed Pearl Harbor. Mom and Dad woke up Monday morning to the news of the attack. That afternoon President Roosevelt signed the Declaration of War against Japan which Congress passed with only one dissenting vote in both houses.

Tuesday morning there were long lines at the enlistment office at the Federal Building on Noble Street. Ben called Dad and said he was going to enlist. They both lined up at the enlistment office Wednesday morning. Turned out, the day that my father slid into second base and tore up his right knee kept him out of the Army. The doctor at the enlistment center stamped Dad's enlistment paper "Medically Disqualified". Dad was depressed for weeks afterward. He and Ben had hoped to be assigned to the same military unit. Dad's contribution to the war effort would be the cotton cloth made in the mill.

Ben got selected for officer candidate school and became a Second Lieutenant in the infantry. On November 8, 1942, as Mom and Dad were attending services at the First Methodist Church, Ben was one of the thousands of American and British troops landing in the cities of Casablanca, Oran, and Algiers in North Africa. He was decorated for his leadership and promoted during the North African campaign. The day after I was born on July 9, 1943, Ben was one of the 150,000 infantry troops who took part in the sunrise amphibious assault on the southern shores of Sicily. As his unit moved across the island, he was shot in the leg. It wasn't a serious wound, but it did get him placed on a plane back to England. After recovering in the hospital, he was placed in a pool of replacements who would be sent to fill openings in units.

On June 6, 1944, Ben led his unit onto the beach on D-Day. He then fought across France and helped liberate Paris and marched in the American Forces Parade down the Champs Elysees. Germany surrendered on May 7, 1945.

After the end of the war in Europe, Ben was on a ship that pulled into New York harbor on the first of August. Dad picked him up at the train station two days later, but Ben was no longer the jovial, happy-go-lucky man who Dad had watched go off to the military in 1941. He came home a different person. Dad said he had a shadow on his soul.

CHAPTER 4

As we finished our meals and continued to cruise across the Atlantic my chatty neighbor continued to make small talk.

"So, how'd you get the nickname 'Right Hand'?"

"Not a remarkably interesting story, truth be told. I started first grade in the fall of 1949. My best friend George Daniel Franklin lived one block from my house, and I got into the same class. The first day of school we made a new friend, JB Farkenfield. When our teacher, Mrs. Burns, told the class to put our right hands over our hearts while we recited the Pledge of Allegiance, I put my left hand over my heart. I'm left-handed so to me that was my right hand or to be grammatically correct, my correct hand.

Condescendingly Mrs. Burns told me, 'Use your other hand,' and all the children laughed. Later that day JB gave me the nickname Right Hand and it stuck. Mrs. Burns tried to keep me from writing with my left hand. She would come by my desk and take the pencil out of my left hand and place it in my right hand. When she walked away I would put it back in my left hand.

George, JB, and I became the three musketeers, but I was the only one in their right mind. We ran the mountains together, played baseball together, went to church together and when we got older, we chased girls together. I was the only left-handed pitcher on the high school team. The coach thought it was a hoot his left-handed pitcher was called Right Hand.

"Sounds like an ideal life," Art commented.

"Yes, I guess it was. It was after the war and people were building families, buying houses and cars. During our junior year in high school, Mr. Rhoades, my neighbor, asked me if I wanted a wooden ski boat that he had built in his garage from plans from *Mechanics Illustrated* magazine. His wife was after him to get it out of the garage so she could park her car in the garage rather than out on the street. They were expecting their second child, and he couldn't afford to buy a motor, so he was willing to give it to me to get it out of the garage and bring peace with his wife.

George Daniel and JB helped me move the boat over to my house and put it in the backyard. We found an old boat trailer for sale for $25 and the man threw in a hitch. George Daniel had a 1940 Ford, so we put the hitch on his car. We loaded the boat on the trailer and took it to Geoge Daniels house because they had a three-car garage, and we could store the boat in one of the garage spaces. We found a used Mark 58A 45 HP Mercury outboard motor with the controls and steering wheel. The three of us pooled our money and bought it.

For the next two months we worked on that boat every free moment that we had. We installed hardware, running lights and a windshield. Our last purchase was a set of water skis, tow rope, and a ski belt. The first weekend in May, we took the boat to Lake Washataw to try it out and to teach ourselves to water ski. The 45 HP Mercury made the lightweight wooden boat fly across the water. By the end of the day about all we had accomplished was to get sunburned. JB could almost stay up for two minutes before falling. George Daniel and I would get up and then fall before we had skied twenty feet.

We were back on the water the next weekend and after much effort we all got where we could stay up until we got tired and let go of the rope. We also got an old truck inner tube which we tied to the tow rope. One of us would sit on the inner tube while the driver of the boat tried to sling us off. That summer we started taking dates up to the lake to ski. We found a place we named 'Hanky Panky Cove' where we spread our blankets on the grass and made out with the girls when we weren't skiing. George Daniel had a girlfriend that he had liked since we were in fifth grade. JB and I took whoever would say yes when we asked them for a date."

Laughing, Art replied, "I can relate to that. Wasn't much of a ladies man in my teenage years, not that I'm any more of one now."

It appeared Art was talked out, at least for a while, but his prodding me to conversation had brought up some memories I hadn't recalled in a long time.

JB's mother was the French teacher at the high school and taught summer school every year. She encouraged him to take a class every summer while George and I worked at Collins Drug Store. George ran the soda fountain and I worked with Mr. Collins filling prescriptions. Because of going to summer school for three years, JB was able to enroll at Auburn for the winter quarter of 1961. He had completed his freshman year by the time George Daniel, and I started at Auburn in September.

In late August, JB was home after completing summer quarter. The three musketeers decided to make one last visit to Hanky Panky Cove before starting college. I had a date with a girl who went to Oxford High School and would be going to Auburn in September. JB had a date with a girl he met at the local hangout the night before. George was with Glenda, the only girl he had ever dated. For eight years they had been boyfriend and girlfriend, and everyone expected them to be married someday. While JB and I, and our dates, were off in the boat to show the girls the dam, George and Glenda consummated their love.

In September, the three musketeers went off to Auburn and the love of George's life went to Agnes Scott Women's College in Atlanta. Glenda wanted to go to Auburn, but her mother had insisted that she attend Agnes Scott where she had gone to school. George and I were roommates and he called her almost every day and wrote her letters every night. Quite suddenly, in October Glenda stopped taking his calls and writing him letters.

George called Glenda's best friend and asked her if she knew why Glenda would not take his phone calls and didn't write to him. When George walked back into our room after hanging up the phone at the other end of the hall, he looked like death warmed over. He was sobbing as he sat down on the edge of his bed.

"What's the matter George?" I had never seen George cry and prepared myself for the worst news.

Wiping the tears from his eyes he told me, "I got Glenda pregnant, Right. It was for sure an accident, not that we didn't figure on having a family someday, just not now."

"George, I'm sorry, but you'll do the right thing by her, and things will work out," I offered hopefully.

"Right, she didn't keep the baby, she had an abortion, and her mother has forbidden her to talk to me."

"Damn, George. Maybe just give her a little time? I'm sure she'll come around and talk to you. Hell, y'all have been together since fifth grade. I know she loves you. Just give it some time."

Time didn't solve the problem. Glenda never talked to George again and she broke George's heart. Four years later I read a marriage announcement in the *Anniston Star* that she married an engineer from Georgia Tech.

Meanwhile, Art had picked up a section of the paper I had finished reading and started back up on conversing, "Damn thing. Reading an article about some of the guys who came back from Vietnam. Not sure how we got into the mess in the first place but looks like some of these guys will never be the same."

I nodded in agreement as he continued. "I couldn't serve. Got medically discharged before I got out of boot camp."

"What happened, if you don't mind me asking?"

"Shot my own damn self in the leg. Not on purpose, even though that's what some thought at the time. I just never handled a gun, and they were rushing us through training wanting to send us off to hell as quick as possible. That probably saved my life. How about you? Did you serve?"

"Not in combat. In 1961 when the three musketeers went off to the Alabama Polytechnic Institute, soon to become Auburn University, no one was worrying about being drafted into the Army. But JB's father worked for the Army and saw a war coming in Southeast Asia. He told us a war would start before we could graduate. He told us repeatedly, 'You don't want to be drafted into the Army to fight in the jungles. Take my advice and sign up for Air Force ROTC.'

It wasn't a big decision for JB and George Daniel because they both wanted to be pilots, but I wanted to be a pharmacist and come back to Anniston and work in Collins Drug Store, so I was reluctant to follow the advice. After some peer pressure from the other two, I got in the Air Force ROTC line at registration. At the end of our sophomore year, we took the Officer Qualification test and got accepted into Advanced Air Force ROTC which led to us being commissioned Second Lieutenants at graduation. It was a good thing I had followed the advice to join ROTC because the war was going into its second year and the draft was in full swing. Those classmates who sang 'Mickey Mouse, ROTC' in 1961 were now looking for ways to avoid being drafted. Some of our classmates got into the National Guard while a few headed to Canada rather than serve in the Army when they got their draft notices."

"So, if you didn't see jungle duty, what did you do? How about your buddies?" Art asked. By this time, I had to admit, having a good listener made the long flight more tolerable.

"Well, during George Daniel's orientation flight at ROTC camp, the summer after our junior year, he had a medical problem during the flight, and he was medically disqualified for flight training. This put him into a depressed funk and all he wanted to do was stay drunk. After a good ass kicking by both JB and me he started paying enough attention to his studies that he graduated in 1965 with a degree in law enforcement. He applied and got accepted to the school for new Office of Special Investigation (OSI) agents. I had earned a degree in pharmacy in June 1965 and was commissioned in the Medical Service Corps (MSC). When George finished his OSI school he was assigned to the OSI office at Maxwell.

JB had graduated at the end of the summer quarter in 1964. George and I were groomsmen in his wedding to Pam, a girl he had met at Auburn. When JB told me he had met the girl he was going to marry, I told him that I was looking forward to meeting the girl who caught the nerd who didn't have three dates the whole time he was at Auburn because he was always studying. JB went to flight school and got selected to train to be a pilot of the F-4 Phantom Fighter.

As for myself, after attending basic MSC class at Gunter Air Force Base in Montgomery, Alabama in the fall of 1965, I was assigned to the hospital at Maxwell Air Force Base which was just across town."

CHAPTER 5

"Sounds like you got a prime duty station. Basically, your hometown," Art observed.

"Yes, I got lucky, I reported to work at the hospital on January 2nd. For some stupid reason the military didn't have pharmacists working in hospital pharmacies. I was made the Medical Supply Officer.

Two days later I met a nurse, Lieutenant Sue Mullins, and fell head over heels in love. She was a little package of dynamite. Her perfect body combined with an infectious personality knocked me for a loop. It was love at first sight. George said it was lust at first sight. Whatever it was, I knew I wanted to spend the rest of my life with her. I remember the exact day, April 3rd, when I went to the BX and bought a diamond engagement ring. That night I got down on one knee and asked Sue to marry me. She asked me if I was sure I wanted to get married since we had only been dating for a little over two months. I told her I wanted to marry her after the first week."

"Did she say yes?" Art asked.

"Yep, she did, but on one condition, that we meet each other's families before we set a date. Sue was from Birmingham, so we drove up to her parent's house the next Saturday. Her dad and mom weren't very enthusiastic about the engagement. After that cool reception, I was glad when we left to drive over to Anniston to visit my parents. My parents were more receptive to getting a daughter-in-law. I think it was because Mom thought that I would never get married.

We were married in the chapel at Maxwell Air Force Base on June 4th exactly six months after we first met. Our families in Anniston and Birmingham came to the wedding. George Daniel was a groomsman in the wedding. JB couldn't come because he was training in F-4s at MacDill Air force Base, in Tampa, Florida. We got back from our honeymoon trip and found that George had moved out of the apartment we were sharing and into the BOQ on base."

"So, were you Stateside for your entire tour of duty?" Art asked.

"No, when George and I first came on active duty we had requested an assignment to Japan but got assigned to Maxwell, the closest Air Force base to our hometown and to Auburn. We had hoped to see the world on the government's dime, but we were stuck in our backyards. As soon as Sue and I got back from our honeymoon trip to Panama City Beach, she changed her assignment request to match mine. The assignment god must have been looking out for us because two weeks later we got orders to report to Misawa AFB, Japan at the end of September. Misawa's on the northern tip of the main island of Honshu. It has cold, snowy winters and we were both excited about playing in the snow and experiencing a different culture.

About that same time JB called to let me know that he would finish his F-4 training at MacDill at the end of July and he was being assigned to the new F-4 wing that was being activated at Misawa to replace the F-100 wing that had been sent to Vietnam He and Pam got there about the 5th of September."

"So, two of the three musketeers were reunited?" Art observed.

"Actually, all three of us ended up in Japan. The second week of July George got orders assigning him to the OSI office at Tachikawa Air Force Base, Japan which is just outside of Tokyo.

I don't know what it was like for those guys, but leaving home to see the world was kind of bittersweet. The last Saturday in August, the hospital had a farewell party for Sue and me at the O Club. I had bought a new VW Bug just before we got married and we were going to ship it to Misawa. We drove up to Anniston to visit my folks before we flew to Japan and then we drove over to

Birmingham to say goodbye to Sue's family. We had to take the Bug to New Orleans to put it on a ship that would transport it to Misawa. About five miles outside of Birmingham, Sue started to cry. I asked her what was wrong, and she said, 'I won't see my family for the next three years.' That's when it sunk in for me too.

The only way we'd have to communicate with our families was by mail that went by slow boat from Japan to San Francisco. A letter would take about a month to get to Alabama. Shortwave radio from the MARS station could connect you with a shortwave radio operator in the States who could then make a phone call, but you had to get on a waiting list to try to make a call. In three years, we got through once for a three-minute call.

By the time we got to New Orleans, Sue was cried out and was again excited about our adventure. We got a hotel room at the Hotel Royal which is a block from Bourbon Street and a three-minute walk to the French Market. After putting the Bug on the ship, we spent the rest of the day sightseeing. We stopped at Cafe du Monde for coffee and beignets. We ate at Brennan's Restaurant in the French Quarter and had their iconic dessert, Bananas Foster. That night we hit the famous spots along Bourbon Street including Preservation Hall for an hour of jazz, then made our way to Pat O'Brien's and ordered a Hurricane. There was a piano player who could play any song that a customer could name. She kept the place jumping. We staggered back to our hotel at 1:30 and fell into bed. Our flight to San Francisco didn't take off until 3 PM so we went to the Jazz Brunch at the Court of Two Sisters.

The time difference had us in San Francisco at 4:30 and we took a cab from the airport to the Marines Memorial Club in downtown. The Club served only active duty and retired military members, and it was near impossible to get a reservation with all the military going through San Francisco in 1966 to catch planes to Vietnam. Fortunately, Sue's father had been a Marine in WWII and was a member of the club. He always stayed there when he was in San Francisco on business. Our World Airways charter flight took off at 11 PM the next night for Yokota Air Force Base Japan with a stop in Anchorage, Alaska."

"Sounds like you enjoyed your last few days Stateside," Art said.

"We sure made the most of it," I agreed.

I realized that between the two of us I was actually the talkative one. Funny thing how Art got me talking about my life with just a couple of questions.

Our flight was nearly over, and Art didn't seem interested in hearing any more of my life story, so I settled in and thought about the time Sue and I arrived at the terminal at Yokota, Japan.

We were greeted by Tech. Sgt. Bernard who had been my NCOIC (Noncommissioned Officer in Charge) of the medical warehouse at Maxwell before he got orders for Tachikawa. He had been in Japan long enough that his new Buick had arrived and he gave us a ride to the family transient quarters.

"Your flight up to Misawa will be on Air America Wednesday morning," Bernard explained. "My wife and I would like to take you out to dinner tomorrow night, our treat. We found a Kobe beef steakhouse that we want to try."

When Sue and I got to our room, we didn't take time to undress before we fell into the bed and went right off to sleep.

The next evening TSgt. Bernard and his wife took us to a fancy restaurant and ordered the most expensive steaks on the menu. When we got ready to leave he pulled out a wad of yen and paid the bill. When we got back to our room Sue asked, "Where does a tech sergeant get the money to buy a new Buick and afford to eat Kobe beef?"

"Maybe he has family money," I suggested, but the entire encounter had me feeling that something wasn't right.

The next morning, we caught the Air America flight up to Misawa and were met by JB and Pam as we walked down the stairs to the tarmac.

"Looks like marriage agrees with you," I said, hugging JB and giving Pam a kiss on the cheek.

They drove us to the Housing Office, and we were able to secure on-base housing next door to them.

JB's F-4 wing was being delayed because of modifications that had to be made to the planes, so he wasn't doing much flying. In

October he got orders to report to a F-4 wing in Vietnam in January. He and Pam left on the first of December to fly back to the States before JB had deploy to Vietnam. At about the same time George Daniel arrived at Tachikawa for his new Job.

I was working the day shift and Sue was working nights on the med-surg ward, so we didn't have much time to spend together. In December we both had a day off at the same time, and the first week in March it was confirmed that Sue was pregnant. The military policy at the time was that if a woman was pregnant she could not stay on active duty, so Sue was discharged.

I called the OSI office at Tachi to tell George the good news but the person who answered the phone said he was TDY to a classified location. When George returned he called me.

"Right, I've got good news and bad news. The bad news is JB has been shot down and is listed as missing in action. They suspect he's been captured but haven't gotten confirmation from the Red Cross."

"Lord, that's awful news. Pam's still in the States so we hadn't heard about JB." Stunned by the news, I said, more to myself than to George Daniel, "He must be MIA; he must have ejected. We must keep thinking that way. Sue and I will keep him in our prayers." We were quiet for a few moments, not able to fully digest what it would mean for us to experience a future as husbands and fathers without JB by our sides. "So, I could use that good news now, George Daniel."

"Yeah, well, the good news is I'm getting married!"

"Excellent. It's about time you settled down. Tell me about her."

"Her name is Sashiko Ryoshi. We met while I was at Wakkanai Air station working undercover. Obviously, she's Japanese. She's also a college graduate and speaks perfect English. The formal wedding will be on June 6th at Wakkanai. You and Sue must come."

I assured George we'd be at the wedding, and I gave him our good news about the baby due in September. After we ended our call I sat for a long time contemplating JB's fate. He was a tough guy and if he survived the ejection and was taken prisoner by the

Vietcong, he'd be in a world of misery, but at least he'd be alive. We were so close, all but blood brothers, and I just knew if he was dead, I'd feel some kind of void in my heart.

CHAPTER 6

As our plane began its descent into Helsinki my anxiety returned. I was on the other side of the world from my family. For what? My first obligation was to my wife and son, but what I had embarked on could jeopardize my ability to be there for them. There were few times in my life when we'd been apart since Sue delivered our son Herbert Albert Talbert, 8 lbs. 12 oz., on September 14, 1967.

Herbert Albert Talbert (say that three times real fast) was immediately nicknamed "HAT". No one could believe we named our child Herbert Albert Talbert, but he was named after our grandfathers, Herbert Talbert, and Albert Mullins. In our defense, Sue was under the effects of the drugs she had been given during childbirth and I was drunk from all the congratulatory toasts from the gang in the Officer's Club bar. In hindsight, it would have been better if we had waited till the next day to fill out the paperwork that had to be sent to the American Consulate to record our son's birth.

Japan is a beautiful country with a rich culture. Sue and I enjoyed the time we spent there, and it wasn't without drama. We survived a blizzard that closed all the flight lines in the Tokyo area, leaving only our runways in Misawa open. We were given two hours notice to expand our 24-bed hospital to its 100-bed maximum capacity in order to receive a diverted AC-141 air evac plane from Vietnam with 97 patients on board. Sue and other wives who were nurses put on their uniforms and went to work. Through the extraordinary effort of many people from all over the base, both military and civilian volunteers, we were ready to receive the patients from Vietnam.

On Thursday morning, May 16, 1968, I was in my office talking to a new airman who had just arrived on the Wednesday Air America flight. Suddenly, the whole building started to move. My desk was jumping up and down and the large file cabinets fell over. I quickly gathered some important documents from my desk and said, "Let's get out of here before the building falls down on us."

We made it outside, but we could not keep our footing. The ground was heaving in two-foot waves. I watched in horror as the ground opened and swallowed a huge pine tree. Large American cars were being bounced around like rubber balls and light poles were breaking. The earthquake went on for 12 minutes and eventually was recorded as 7.8 on the Richter scale.

Downtown Misawa was on fire. Train tracks were twisted like pretzels and the road up to the northside of the base was destroyed by a landslide and was impassable. After taking an assessment of the damage to the hospital and ensuring that no one was injured, I got in my Bug and drove to my quarters to check on Sue and HAT. All the wives and children were in their front yards and our quarters looked like they had taken a direct hit from a bomb. A few minutes later, a tsunami warning was issued, and we were ordered to move to higher ground About an hour later, the all-clear announcement was made.

We suffered through major aftershocks for days and it took weeks for the base to get power, running water and the sewage back online. Civil Engineers inspected all the buildings and put tar paper over the gaping holes. We were told we could move back into our quarters but if another big quake hit to get out as fast as possible because the building would probably collapse. I went upstairs and dragged our mattress down to the living room. We slept in our clothes right next to the front door so we could get out quickly. About a week after we started sleeping in the house, a strong aftershock woke us up and we ran outside. One of our neighbors was standing in the yard holding her child. She was naked. Unlike Sue and I, she didn't sleep in her clothes.

In July, I was notified that I had been selected to augment the Fifth Air Force Medical IG Team inspecting the hospitals in Korea. I called George and asked him if Sue and HAT could stay with them for the two weeks I would be in Korea. Sashiko was ecstatic to have Sue and HAT as guests. It was good for our mental health to get away from Misawa for two weeks. When we got back to Misawa, we moved out of our tar-paper shack into a newly renovated unit.

CHAPTER 7

As 1968 turned into 1969, Sue and I were marking off the days until we moved back home to Alabama. In February the Air Force offered me a permanent commission which meant that I would be a career officer. I turned it down. George also had been selected for a permanent commission and he had accepted, planning to make the Air Force a career.

On May 16th, there was a Great Shakes Day anniversary party at the O Club. The featured drink was a Librium Cocktail in recognition of all the tranquilizers taken to settle nerves after last year's earthquake. It was a good thing our quarters were less than a block from the club because I could not have driven home. The party was a good release valve after a year of tension of worrying about having another big quake. Even after a year, there were people who still slept in their clothes down on the first floor.

The first week of June I had to go TDY (Temporary Duty Travel) to Tachikawa to augment the 5th Air Force Medical Inspector General Team while it inspected the hospital. At the beginning of the year, the Air Force had implemented a policy to have its hospitals inspected for accreditation by the Joint Commission on Accreditation of Hospitals (JCAH). JCAH used the term "medical materiel", so the Air Force changed the name from Medical Supply to Medical Materiel. The Joint Commission also required a registered pharmacist to be in every hospital pharmacy. The wise heads in the Pentagon decided to follow that JCAH guidance and put Registered Pharmacist officers in charge of pharmacies, which is how I found myself inspecting Medical Materiel.

The first day of the inspection my old acquaintance, MSgt. Bernard invited me to his home for dinner. He had been promoted and would soon transfer back to Maxwell to be the Non-Commissioned Officer in Charge (NCOIC) of Medical Materiel. I declined the invitation, pointing out that it would be inappropriate for us to socialize until the inspection was completed.

During my inspection I came across an invoice for new leather furniture that had been purchased for the Hospital commander's office. The price for a couch and two chairs seemed exceedingly high to me, so I flagged in for the IG.

When the inspection finished up and I was due to head back to Misawa, I met MSgt. Bernard for lunch at his house off base. Suddenly, a light bulb lit and red flags started flying in my head. I made quick work of the lunch and rushed back to the hospital to call George Daniel and asked if he could see me. I told him I suspected something was wrong with the amount paid for some custom-made furniture.

When I got to George's office, I explained what I suspected. "George, something fishy is going on at Medical Material and it's not just a problem for the IG's JCAH accreditation." I explained how Sgt. Bernard met Sue and I when we arrived in Japan and wondered about his ability to afford a new Buick and treat us to a high-end meal on a Sargent's salary.

"Maybe he or his wife's family has money." George Daniel suggested.

"That's what I told Sue at the time. Maybe that's the case, and we should check that with someone Stateside, but I don't think so. I could be wrong, but he's living in the largest house in what they call 'Little America'. He has a yard man and I saw a maid and a Japanese cook. He has a leather living room set and a rosewood dining table that could seat 12 people. From all appearances he's living way above what a Master Sergeant could afford. I think it's worth you check this out, George." I pulled a copy of the suspicious invoice out of my pocket and handed it to George.

He studied it for a minute and said, "Okay, let's pay a visit to this shop that made the furniture."

It didn't take George long, with his fluent Japanese, to get the shop owner to admit that Sergeant Bernard had told him to overcharge the hospital for one living room set and give him a second set of furniture for "free".

George promptly called the local police, who had jurisdiction on any crimes committed off-base, and they took a sworn statement from the shop owner.

On a Sunday night two Security Policemen observed a man trying to open the door to a warehouse where excess war readiness medical supplies were stored. When they approached him, he ran but they caught him. After being interviewed by the OSI he confessed that he had bought the key to the warehouse from MSgt. Bernard and that Bernard was selling medical supplies on the black market. This led George Daniel, the OSI, and Japanese police to bust the largest black-market ring in military history, up until that time. MSgt. Bernard was reduced in grade to airman basic and sentenced to 30 years in Leavenworth Military Prison.

In July my travel and separation orders arrived, and I officially became FIGMO (fuck it got my orders). We flew down to Tachi on the 14th of September and spent the night with George and Sashiko before flying out of Yokota the next day. We landed at Travis Air Force Base in Fairfield, California only two hours after we left Yokota because of the international date line.

I was processed out at the personnel office. They took our ID cards, gave me my discharge, a DD214 form, paid me my last paycheck, and gave me a voucher for plane tickets to my home of record. When we got on the bus heading for the airport in San Francisco, I was a civilian for the first time in four years and I was looking forward to going to work at Collins Drug Store.

When we got to Anniston, we rented an apartment while we looked for a house to buy. I went to work at the drug store as a pharmacist and Sue took a job at Northeast Alabama Regional

Hospital. We joined the First United Methodist Church, where I had been baptized when I was 12 years old, and every Sunday you would find us sitting in the third pew on the left with my mother and father.

When Sue and I were discharged from active duty, we kept our Reserve commissions and joined the Reserves which earned us points towards a military retirement. We couldn't find positions in a Reserve unit, so we became Individual Mobilization Augmentees (IMA) in the Air Force Reserves. An IMA is a Ready Reservist assigned to a specific position within an active-duty unit that is essential during wartime. Sue and I both got positions at Maxwell AFB Hospital. Once a month we drove down to Montgomery for reserve duty. I worked in the pharmacy and Sue worked on the med/surg unit. Every summer we did a two-week training period at the hospital while my mom watched HAT.

Sue and I were happy in small town Anniston. As the years passed, I bought out Mr. Collins and changed the name of the drug store to Right's Pharmacy and Sue moved up in the nursing hierarchy. We were active in our church where I became the Sunday school teacher for the young men's class and a member of the executive board, and Sue worked in the nursery.

CHAPTER 8

Our pilot lowered the landing gear and turned into the base leg of our approach to Helsinki-Vantaa Airport. He reduced power, lowered the flaps and we touched down right on schedule. We were lined up to deplane when Art asked me, "Hey, I never asked, but what will you be doing in Helsinki? Are you here on business?"

I had neglected to prepare an explanation that wouldn't give away my real reason for being in Finland and my pause seemed to arouse Art's curiosity.

"Oh, okay. If you're here on some secret spy mission, I don't want you to tell me. You'd have to kill me, right, Right?" he laughed as we moved forward down the aisle.

Art and I said our goodbyes at baggage claim. I picked up my backpack from the luggage turnstile and went out to the reception area. A man was holding up a placard with two names, one of which was mine. I walked up to him and introduced myself. He offered no introduction, but explained we were waiting for the other traveler. After a few minutes another man with a backpack joined us. Our driver led us outside through the parking garage to an old Saab. He stowed our heavy backpacks in the trunk and with no fanfare or conversation he drove east from Helsinki to an area that appeared to be near the border with the USSR. He parked the Saab in an unpaved clearing and got out of the car. Opening the trunk, he handed us our backpacks, a trenching tool, a compass, and a crude map.

"See that?" he said, pointing to a barb-wired fence about fifty yards away, "That's the border. Use this to dig under the fence.

We have been observing the area for a month and there hasn't been any activity from the Russians. We don't think this area has landmines. We have thrown rocks into the area and there have been no explosions."

Hearing that sent my anxiety level soaring. I glanced at my fellow traveler who was listening intently and looked cool as a cucumber, as if our friend was reciting the box scores from the last Yankees game.

Our driver continued, "You don't have to worry about being stopped by Finnish Border Guard patrols. The captain in command of this sector is a friend of ours. The Russian border patrols are very predictable, passing by every 45 minutes. Good luck. God is protecting you."

With that he got into the Saab and drove back the way we came. I stood rooted to the ground, not sure of what I was doing here or what to do next.

My companion started to move toward the fence, and I followed. "This isn't my first trip into the USSR. Just follow me and do what I tell you and we'll be fine," he explained.

With every step closer to the border, my heart beat faster. As we hid in the dense brush waiting for the Russian patrol, I was sure that my pounding heart could be heard by anyone within fifty yards. Five minutes after the Russian patrol passed, we dug our way under the fence with the trenching tool and backfilled the trench, covering it with a layer of leaves and twigs to mask our entry point. We made a mad dash across the border, and every time my feet hit the ground I expected to be blown up by a landmine. Using our maps and compass, we hiked through the forest as the sun was setting. We buried our trench tools in the heavy undergrowth which my companion marked with a cross made of twigs. When we reached a grove of tall trees, we heard someone say "Revelation". My companion offered the correct replay, "3:2." I recalled reading that Brother Andrew said he felt a call to respond to Jesus' words in Revelation 3:2, *Wake up! Strengthen what remains and is about to die, for I have found your deeds unfinished in the sight of God.*

We quickly turned over our heavy backpacks, each laden with 100 Bibles, to the Russian Christians. We retraced our steps, retrieved our trenching tools, dug ourselves back to the Finnish side of the border, filled the hole under the fence and covered it with leaves. When we were safely in the cover of the forest on the Finnish side, I felt so weak I had to sit down against a tree.

In June 1981, I told my friends I was going on a Church Mission to the Philippines. During Chairman Mao's bloody Cultural Revolution in 1976, Christian churches and Bibles were destroyed. Christians wrote down Bible verses they had memorized and passed them to other Christians. In 1980 a Christian woman by the name of Mama Kwang secretly contacted Open Doors and requested they smuggle Bibles into China.

"Project Rainbow", the largest operation so far for Open Doors, smuggled 30,000 New Testaments into China. The volunteers who carried the heavy suitcases overland from the new Territories, jokingly called it "Operation Hernia."

Mama Kwang was very thankful for the New Testaments, but she needed 1,000,000 Bibles to spread the word of Jesus throughout China. A project of that magnitude would cost millions of dollars and be fraught with danger. Anyone who was caught would die in a Chinese prison.

After much prayer, Open Doors agreed to take on the project. "Operation Pearl" raised millions of dollars from Christians around the world. One million Bibles written in Chinese characters were printed in San Francisco and shipped to Hong Kong, where they were stored, waiting to be smuggled into China. A large barge was secured, and the Bibles were loaded onboard.

The organizers needed a tugboat to pull the barge, but one willing to risk the trip into Chinese waters off the coast of Shantou, China could not be found in Hong Kong. Two new tugboats for sale in Singapore were purchased at rock-bottom prices because the company that ordered them had gone bankrupt.

I joined nineteen other Christians in Hong Kong to be the crew. Many of us had never sailed before and on the first day of sailing through rough seas, several crew members joined me along the rail, throwing up last night's meal. Under cover of night on June 18th the barge was pulled to within a few dozen feet of the beach. Crew members were on constant alert watching for a communist patrol boat and listening for an alarm from the Army coast watchers.

There were a thousand Christian faithful waiting to bring the Bibles ashore. The Bibles, packed in watertight boxes, were pushed over the side of the barge and people from shore waded out into the water to retrieve them. With the constant fear of being seen by the Chinese Navy or Army Shore Watchmen, we unloaded over 11,000 cartons of Bibles in just under two hours. Little did we know, the Army Shore Watchmen who were manning the watchtower near the beach had been drinking and were so drunk they passed out and were fast asleep.

As the last box containing 90 Bibles was pushed over the side, the barge and the tugs began receding into the distance. God was watching over us. Back in Hong Kong after the successful operation, the smugglers boarded planes bound for homes around the world. I went back to the quiet life of Anniston, where no one had any idea the pharmacist at Right's Pharmacy was an international smuggler.

CHAPTER 9

When I reflected on my experience with Open Doors, it left me feeling satisfied. I had done more than just write a check. There were people in this world who would know the story and the love of Jesus Christ because of the work that I did. My faith and my family were stronger than ever.

With each passing year, HAT grew more athletic and played most sports. Like his great grandfather, grandfather, and father before him he particularly excelled in baseball. By the time he was in high school he stood 6'3" tall, weighed 210 hard-muscled pounds, and threw a fastball that was clocked at 95 MPH and a curve that broke about a foot. There was only one reason he would not get a full ride to a major college or be drafted by the pros; his control was terrible. When HAT let the ball go, it was anybody's guess where it might end up. His walks to strikeouts ratio turned the scouts away.

The summer he graduated from high school Bill Abrams, the coach of the Blue Mountain Bombers, the local American Legion team, asked him to pitch for his team. Bill had been a major league pitcher, and he was sure he could correct HAT's wildness. By the end of the summer, HAT's fastball was clocked at 96 mph, his curveball was sharp, and he had added a change-up, but most importantly, he had control of his pitches.

A scout from Jefferson State Junior College saw HAT pitch a two hitter against the Bessemer Steel Men on the 4th of July and offered HAT a scholarship. At the end of August, HAT loaded up his pickup truck and drove over to Jefferson State and became a member of the Pioneer baseball team. During the next two years HAT led the Pioneers to two state junior college championships and trips to the national tournament. By the start of the second season, scouts from the pros and major colleges were sitting in the stands at his games and he was drafted in the fourth round by the Minnesota Twins.

Rather than turn pro, he signed a letter of intent to play for the Auburn Tigers coached by Hal Baird after considering scholarships to three SEC colleges: Vanderbilt, Mississippi State, and Auburn. I was pleased that HAT would be the third generation of Talberts to attend the "loveliest village on the plains".

HAT had a successful season his junior year at Auburn. During his senior year he threw two no-hitters, and the team went to the NCAA tournament. The pro scouts had been attending all his games and HAT's name was way up on the list of prospects. He graduated from Auburn with a BS degree in Physical Education and was drafted ninth in the first round of the June 5th pro draft by the California Angels who then traded his rights to Detroit before the day was out.

Three days after Auburn was eliminated from the NCAA tournament a scout of the Tigers showed up at our house in Golden Springs with a contract for $1,000,000 dollars for three years and $300,000 as a signing bonus. HAT didn't have an agent and probably could have gotten more if he had signed with one. After the family lawyer looked over the contract, HAT signed on the dotted line and deposited the $300,000 in the First National Bank of Anniston. The next day HAT loaded up his pickup, kissed his mother goodbye, shook my hand, and drove up to Hillyer High Road to tell a special girl goodbye. After she promised to write, he told her he would call when he got to Lakeland.

After nine hours he arrived in Lakeland, Florida to join the Lakeland Tigers of the Florida State League. HAT tore up the league, pitching a no hitter on July 12th. With a record of 5 wins, no losses and one no decision, he was called into the manager's office on the 15th and told he was being moved up to Double A.

He was given a plane ticket to London, Ontario, Canada and told he had to be there to start the Sunday afternoon game. When he got back to his apartment, he called me to tell me he was being sent to London.

"Do they play baseball in England?"

"No Dad, not London, England. London, Ontario, Canada, the Tiger's Double A team."

"Congratulations son, I bet you'll be in the majors next year. Give us a call when you get to Canada and give us your new phone number. I need to let you go; the customers are backing up. Have to keep rolling those pills. Love you bud."

Before cleaning out his apartment and moving his meager possessions into a storage facility, HAT called the special girl on Hillyer High Road and gave her the news. She was excited for him, but she had news of her own. She had just been hired to teach fifth grade at Tenth Street Elementary School starting in September. HAT promised to call her when he got to London and see her when the season ended.

HAT left his pickup in the Tigers spring training facility parking lot. The equipment manager drove him to the airport in Orlando where he caught an Air Canada flight to London, Ontario. It was the first time he had been outside the United States since we came back from Misawa, Japan in 1969 when he was a baby. As he walked towards the terminal building, HAT noticed the distinct difference between Central Florida and Ontario, Canada; the air didn't feel like a heavy blanket. He wasn't sweating from 90-degree heat with humidity to match.

After picking up his luggage HAT walked to the cab stand and got a taxi. When he told the driver he wanted to go to Labatt Memorial Park, the driver said, "The Tigers are in town for a four-game home stand, and I have tickets for the Sunday afternoon game against the Albany Yankees."

"Well sir, who will you be rooting for?" HAT asked.

Avoiding the question, the driver continued as he looked HAT over in his rear-view mirror, "I bet you don't know that Labatt

Park is the oldest continually operating baseball park in the world. Dates to 1877.”

“No sir, I didn’t know that. I’m Herbert Talbert, but you can call me HAT. I’m supposed to pitch Sunday. They just brought me up from Lakeland in the Florida State League.”

“This is the first season we’ve had a pro team in years. I read about you in the paper this morning. We sure can use some pitching. I think we have the weakest pitching staff in the Eastern League. I know Coach Chambliss will be glad to see you. He’s not having a good year in his first year as a manager.” That would change in 1990 when Chambliss won the outstanding minor league manager award and London won the Eastern League championship.

The taxi stopped at the players entrance, and the driver jumped out to help HAT with his luggage. As HAT looked at the stadium, he noticed what looked like a new blue and orange stripe and tiger heads painted on the stadium walls.

“How much do I owe you?”

“This ride is on me. If you would autograph a ball for my son, that would be enough payment.”

“You got it, see you Sunday.”

HAT walked up to the gate at the players entrance where a sleepy looking old man sat. “Are you the pitcher from Lakeland?” he asked.

“Yes sir, I am him.”

“The dressing room and the manager’s office are through that door,” he said, pointing the way.

As HAT walked into the clubhouse, the familiar smell of sweat welcomed him.

“You must be the superman from Lakeland everybody is talking about,” said a stout, balding man while offering his hand. “I’m Ted Murphy, the assistant equipment manager. Grab any one of the empty lockers. If you don’t have a padlock, I’ll give you one.”

While HAT stowed his gear Ted continued, “You get three uniforms. You know the drill about turning in your dirty uniform after the game so they can be washed. The manager doesn’t like it if you wear a dirty uniform. He wants the team to look like major leaguers even if they don't play like it."

HAT nodded that he understood.

"The team stinks on the field, but we don't want a clubhouse that stinks from keeping dirty uniforms in the lockers. If the manager smells a dirty locker, the locker owner will be fined $25. I know that may not be much for you first-rounders, but it's hard on the guys who didn't get big signing contracts."

Unfortunately, Ted didn't seem to be successful enforcing the dirty locker rule from the aroma that hung heavy in the air.

"The Manager just cut a pitcher who was sharing an apartment with Tony Perez, our backup catcher. Perez is from Puerto Rico, but he speaks English. I'll introduce you to him if you would like to share an apartment. Being a first-rounder, wunderkind, I suppose you may not want to share an apartment, but it's on the bus line so you can ride the bus to the park until your Corvette arrives."

HAT didn't want to begin his time with the team on the wrong foot, but Ted's attitude got under his skin.

"There won't be a Corvette arriving. I own a 1952 Ford pickup that was left to me when my grandpa died. I left it at Tiger Town in Lakeland and will pick it up when the season is over." He paused thinking about what he wanted to say next, "I'm no wunderkind, Ted, just a guy who has been blessed with a strong arm and taught how to control my pitches. I'll talk to Perez about sharing the apartment. I'm sure he can teach me a lot about the hitters."

The apartment was over the garage of a house owned by a widow, Mrs. Hatcher. She had rented it out each winter to students from Western University. When her renters moved out unexpectedly in March, she rented it to Tony and another player from the new professional team. They would move out at the end of August making it available for students again. She also provided meals at a reasonable price and enjoyed having someone to talk with. She took a special attachment to HAT and his Southern drawl.

The hitters were better in the Eastern League, but HAT still finished the season with a 6–2 record and a low ERA. It should have been better, but the relief pitchers gave up leads in two of his starts. Tony Perez brought his average up to 286 in the last month and a half. As roommates and teammates, HAT and Tony spent a lot of time talking about hitters and practicing. Early on, HAT had insisted Tony be his catcher. Normally a manager wouldn't let a pitcher dictate who would be the catcher, but HAT was a first round draft pick, so he gave him a little leeway. As it turned out, it was a successful partnering.

After the last game, the manager called HAT into his office. The good news was that HAT had been invited to spring training with the Detroit Tigers next spring and Tony would be going to spring training with the Toledo Mud Hens, the Triple A team.

The team cleaned out their smelly lockers and Tony and HAT said their goodbyes.

"See you in February, wunderkind. If it gets too cold in Alabama, you can come down to San Juan and stay with me for a few days. I'm playing in the Caribbean Winter League."

HAT clasped his teammate's shoulder, "I just might do that, Tony. Thanks for all your help. I owe you for my success here in London."

After saying goodbye to Mrs. Hatcher and promising to stay in touch, HAT flew to Orlando. He haggled with a taxi driver who agreed to drive him to Tiger Town in Lakeland for $100.

His pickup hadn't been driven in over a month and it didn't surprise HAT that it didn't start. He got out of the truck and stood there looking frustrated when one of the crew who worked at Tiger Town drove up.

"You wouldn't happen to have a set of jumper cables and be willing to give me a jump?" HAT asked, "My battery's dead, she hasn't been driven since I got called up to London on the 16th of July."

"Just so happens that I do. Pop your hood and I'll hook you up. You're HAT, aren't you? Lakeland sure missed you. How did you do in Canada?"

"I went 6–2 and got an invite to Detroit's spring training camp."

"Nice! Hit your starter when I rev up my engine," the good samaritan said as he hopped into his truck.

HAT's truck fired up on the first try.

"My name is Jerry Pearson. I expect I'll see you in February when the pitchers report."

"Nice to meet you, Jerry. Thanks for the jump. I'm sure we'll see each other in the spring. I'll buy you a beer then for the jump. Right now, I'm in a hurry to get home. There's a girl I have a date with tomorrow night."

HAT cleaned out his storage facility and loaded it in his pickup and headed towards Anniston for a reunion with his parents and the special schoolteacher. He looked forward to watching some Auburn football games. Everyone said that Coach Dye had a good team and they expected them to win the SEC.

He also wanted to visit our best friends, JB and Selma Farkenfield. They were like his aunt and uncle. JB and Selma owned a crop-dusting company in Chocwataw County, Alabama. JB had survived his ejection when he was shot down in Vietnam. Pam never returned to Japan, staying in the States and divorcing JB while he spent time as a guest in the Hanoi Hilton. JB left the Air Force in 1974, became an agriculture pilot and joined an Air Force Reserve unit located at Dannelly Field in Montgomery, Alabama.

JB met Selma when he was in Rhodesia on what was rumored to be a mission for the CIA during the Bush War. Selma was a pilot in the Rhodesian Air Force. It didn't take them long to fall in love and as the war in Rhodesia ended Selma resigned from the Rhodesian Air Force and came to the States. They were married in November of 1978. In 1980, while I was off in China taking part in Operation Rainbow they adopted twin girls, Jane, and Julie, who were like HAT's little sisters. They thought the sun rose and set on HAT.

The fall of 1989 was full of football games, fishing and dove hunting with HAT and JB. HAT filled the remaining time with dates with the cute fifth grade teacher, Stephanie Stevens. He had met Stephanie in the spring at Auburn where she was a senior majoring in elementary education. Her red hair, green eyes and perfect body made him melt every time he saw her.

Stephanie was from Anniston but had gone to a private girls' boarding school, so he didn't know her from high school. After two years at Agnes Scott College, she rebelled against her mother and transferred to Auburn. Her family was country-club rich. Her father owned the large brass foundry in Anniston. Our family was Tyler-Pool-middle-class. Tyler Pool was the municipal pool where the kids who didn't have a pool in their backyards hung out on the sweltering summer days.

The fall flew by, and Christmas was soon over. The pitchers and catchers had to report to Tiger Town on February 12th for spring training. HAT did well but the last week of spring training the manager called him into his office and told him that he was being sent to the minor league camp and would be on the roster of the Toledo Mud Hens.

"We want to see you in some real game situations. If we need pitching help, you'll be brought up," the manager explained.

HAT was disappointed but he looked forward to being on the same team with Tony Perez again. Tony was having a great spring and was the starting catcher for the Mud Hens. HAT loaded his gear into the back of the 1952 Ford pickup and drove to Maumee, Ohio, home of the Toledo Mud Hens.

There was an old motel on Key Street which had been turned into small efficiency apartments and was just down the street from Skelton Stadium where the Mud Hens played their home games. The motel had seen better days and had that worn-out look. It needed a new coat of paint, and the parking lot was full of potholes which would ruin the suspension of your car if you hit them going too fast. The good thing about the place was it was cheap and rented on a week-to-week basis. Most of the players hoped they would not be in Triple A long before being called up to "the show" so this was where most of the players stayed during the season. HAT and Tony had called ahead and reserved a second-floor apartment.

HAT and Tony were the starting battery on opening day before a sold-out crowd of 10,197 screaming fans. HAT pitched a three hitter and Tony went two for three and threw out two Columbus players who were trying to steal. Frank Gilhooley, the Mud Hens broadcaster for station WLQR-FM 1470 told his audience that the combination of Talbert and Perez won the game.

"It has been a long time since we have seen this caliber of players in Toledo. You better get out to the ballpark now because they will be taking the short ride up to Detroit real soon," Frank's deep voice boomed over the airways.

The last week of April the starting catcher on the big club broke his ankle sliding into second base and Tony was called up to Detroit to be the backup catcher.

"Who would have ever thought that I would make it to the bigs before the wunderkind?" Tony joked as he said goodbye to HAT. "I would still be at Double A if you hadn't insisted that I be your catcher. I'm sure you'll be going up soon."

HAT continued to pitch well and endured the long bus rides while Tony was enjoying flying from one major league town to another. The third week of May, a call came from Detroit. A member of the starting rotation had blown out his elbow.

"We need you ready to start the night game of a Saturday double header against the Yankees," the Tiger's manager told HAT.

HAT called us immediately. "I've been called up to the majors and will start the Saturday night game against the Yankees. I'll buy your airline tickets if you want to come watch my first major league game."

When I told Sue that HAT had been called up to the majors, HAT could hear his mother yelling with joy.

"When is he going to pitch? We must be there!" she exclaimed.

"HAT don't buy the tickets just yet; I'll see if I can get someone to cover the store for a few days and call you in the morning."

I hung up and called an old friend who was a retired pharmacist and asked if he could cover for me Friday and Saturday. I then called JB to give him the good news. "Sue and I are going to fly up Friday on Delta and fly back Sunday."

JB's response was emphatic, "No, you aren't. Selma and I will fly the C-47 up there Saturday morning. Meet us at the Anniston Municipal Airport at 7:30 AM and invite up to 20 friends. It's only about four hours flying time to Detroit. Let me know how many you invite so I can make ground transportation arrangements. We wouldn't miss this for anything in this world."

I then got busy calling friends and inviting them to fly up to Detroit. I called HAT's high school coach, his American Legion coach, and his coaches from junior college and Auburn, but they were all busy with coaching their teams and couldn't get away. Sue reminded me that I hadn't asked the fifth-grade teacher.

"Who are you talking about?" I asked, "Why would I call his fifth-grade teacher?"

"Not HAT's fifth-grade teacher. Stephanie Stevens. You know, the girl he has been dating since the spring of his senior year at Auburn."

"Oh, right!" I laughed. I wasn't totally clueless about my son's romantic interests, but I didn't realize they were still seeing each other. "Right, you spend too much time at the store. I hope you haven't filled all the seats."

I called Stephanie and gave her the news. Turned out I was a little late because HAT had already called her, and she was arranging for a sub so she could leave Friday. She thanked me for my offer to fly up with our group but declined the invitation saying she had already made the travel plans.

After calling Stephanie, HAT also called Mrs. Hatcher, his former landlady, and told her that he had been called up to Detroit.

"I knew you would make the show. I'll come see you play the next time you play against the Toronto Blue Jays."

HAT explained, "We don't play Toronto again until August. If the rotation stays the same, I'll pitch the game on the 8th. I'll reserve box seats behind our dugout for you. They'll be at the Will Call window. I hope to see you then."

Friday afternoon, HAT met Stephanie at the Detroit Metropolitan Airport and they drove to the Dearborn Inn. The

Dearborn Inn dated back to the '30s when Henry Ford commissioned prominent architect Albert Kahn to design the Colonial Revival style building. Five reproduction homes of famous Americans were built on the grounds creating a small colonial village. The hotel had been placed on the National Historic Register only two years before. When they arrived, HAT signed the registration book as Mr. & Mrs. Herbert A. Talbert.

CHAPTER 11

The next morning, HAT drove to the stadium and parked in the players' lot. He showed Stephanie where the wives and girlfriends sat and told her where they would meet after the game. Saturday morning 618 miles south of the Dearborn Inn there were 24 excited people boarding a plane at the Anniston Municipal Airport for a flight to Detroit.

In the cockpit, Selma made her pre-flight announcement, "If everyone would please take a seat we would like to take off at eight o'clock. I'm Selma Farkenfield, your first officer. My loving husband, JB, will be the second officer on this flight. The flying time to Willow Run Airport in Detroit is four hours and fifteen minutes. Jane and Julie, our daughters, will walk through the cabin and ensure that everyone's seat belt is secured. Please keep them buckled during the flight because we expect some turbulence. Thank you for flying with us today."

The next four hours were uneventful, although our anticipation continued to grow. As we sensed a change in altitude and heard the landing gear descending, the excitement reached a crescendo.

Meanwhile, Selma keyed her mic for transmission to the tower. "This is Tango Foxtrot Charlie 47 263 requesting permission to land at Willow Run Airport."

"Tango Foxtrot Charlie 47 263 you are cleared to land on runway 5/23," the air traffic controller responded.

Selma made a perfect landing and taxied to the general aviation terminal where a bus was waiting to carry the group to Tiger stadium. The bus discharged its passengers at the corner of historic Michigan Avenue and Trumbull. The first pro baseball game in Detroit was played on the site on April 28, 1896. The visitors from Anniston stood wide-eyed looking up at Tiger Stadium. The stadium held more spectators than there were people in Anniston. I made my way through the crowd and got in line for the Will Call ticket window. When I made it to the window, I gave them my name.

As the attendant handed me an envelope, she explained, "I have six tickets two rows up from the Tigers team dugout, but the others are spread out along the right field baseline lower deck."

Hot dogs, beers and Cokes were the lunch menu. None of us were interested in the first game which the Yankees won 6–4. Finally, the public address announcer gave the lineup for the second game.

"Starting on the mound for our home team Tigers is number 23, Herbert Talbert, making his first start in the major leagues, and behind the plate will be number 48, Tony Perez."

We were on our feet yelling, Pride almost kept me from breathing as the announcement was made. Sue was jumping up and down, yelling her head off. HAT saw her and tipped his cap to her. During the game, I ate a pizza, two bags of peanuts and drank two large Cokes, as I nervously watched the game. After seven innings, the Tigers had a four-run lead and HAT had given up only two runs, one of which was unearned. Before the next inning began, we watched Sparky Anderson, the longtime manager of the Tigers, walk over to HAT.

"You've done a good job, rookie, but we'll let the closer finish the game for you. I would've taken you out after six innings, but you looked strong, so I let you go an extra inning."

My heart sank for HAT as I watched him walk off the mound to the dugout. He would be denied throwing the winning pitch, but the crowd cheered, and he pumped his fist and waved his cap to the fans.

The Yankees went three up and three down in the top of the eighth and ninth innings. We gathered behind the Tigers dugout and congratulated HAT on winning his first major league game.

As we boarded our bus to take us to our hotel, Sue and I watched HAT and Stephanie walk hand-in-hand from the players' exit. That evening we celebrated long into the next morning, while HAT and Stephanie enjoyed a celebration of their own at the Deerborn Inn.

The C-47 Gooney Bird flew towards Anniston in the early morning hours of Sunday with its happy passengers. I closed my eyes and considered how different this flight was from that first trip I made to Helsinki. Art's face popped into my head, and I wondered where he was and what he was doing. It suddenly occurred to me that I never asked him what kind of business he was in or what he was doing in Finland.

HAT and Tony were roommates again. When the starting catcher came back from the injured list, Tony expected to be sent back down to Toledo, but he was hitting so well he was kept on the roster as the backup catcher. Sparky explained that he would be HAT's regular catcher. That was good news, because he was enjoying the Major League minimum of $90,000 and was not looking forward to going back to minor league pay, long bus rides, and staying in the old motel on Key Street.

On July 2nd, the team traded their starting catcher to the Atlanta Braves for a relief pitcher and two minor leaguers. Tony became the starting catcher, and his minimum salary saved the team almost a million dollars.

While HAT and Tony were both having great rookie seasons in the majors, the summer of 1990 was full of political turmoil in the Middle East. Saddam Hussein, the strongman in Iraq, accused Kuwait of siphoning crude oil from the Ar-Rumaylah oil fields which were located along their common border. On August 2, 1990, he invaded Kuwait and claimed the invasion of Kuwait was justified because it was "an artificial state carved out of the Iraq coast by Western colonialists". Saddam declared that Kuwait was now a province of Iraq. None of that justification had any merit. Kuwait was recognized as a country by Britain under a League of Nations mandate after WWI before Iraq was created. After Saddam's invasion, Saudi Arabia and other Middle East countries asked NATO for assistance to return Kuwait sovereignty. In response to this request, NATO nations started a military buildup called Operation Desert Shield.

On the 8th of August, Mrs. Hatcher was sitting in her reserved seat watching HAT pitch a 4–0 shutout and Tony go two for four with a home run.

On the same morning, JB's squadron of F-16s from Dannelly Field were called up to deploy to Saudi Arabia to be part of the 14th Air Division (Provisional).

As any farmer knows, August is the beginning of a busy last four months of the crop-dusting season. JB could not have been called up at a more inconvenient time, but when your nation calls, you answer. Selma, Julie, and Jane were at Dannelly Field with other family members of crew who were deploying. They kissed JB goodbye and waved as the planes roared down the runway.

JB led his squadron out over the Atlantic where they would meet up with tankers to refill their fuel on their flight to RAF Lakenheath, England. There they would rest up for their flight to Prince Sultan Air Base, Saudi Arabia.

As JB sweltered in the desert, Selma worked 16 hours a day to fulfill their crop dusting contracts and HAT was winning games for Detroit. Stephanie joined HAT in Detroit after school let out in June and stayed until the end of August when she returned to Anniston for the start of the new school year after Labor Day.

CHAPTER 12

On the Friday after Labor Day 1990 a man came into Right's Pharmacy and asked to speak to me. The clerk turned to the back of the store where pharmacists were busy filling prescriptions.

"Right, there's someone here to see you," she announced.

I finished counting out the pills for the script I was working on before looking up. The gentleman was tall, thin, and looked familiar but I couldn't place him. I see hundreds of folks in my work and although I'm good with names, faces aren't my strong suit.

"I'm Robert Talbert. What can I do for you?"

"Right, is there somewhere we can speak in private?" the man replied.

Taken back by the familiarity in using my nickname, I asked, "And, your name is?"

Smiling, in reply he said, "We spent a whole lot of hours on a flight to Helsinki a few years back and you've already forgotten me?"

"Art! I thought I recognized that face, but you know most of what I remember is in profile with you in the window seat. How have you been? You know, I just came back from a trip and was recalling our conversations. How did you know where to find me?"

Without answering my questions, he flashed a badge and ID identifying him as an agent of the Federal Government.

"Well of all the things I thought you might do for a living, that wasn't one of them," I said as I examined the ID more closely. "Is this for real, Art? That's your face but the name reads Gill Maxwell."

"My name is Gill Maxwell. Right, what I need to discuss must be said in private. Is there somewhere we can talk?"

Confused, I said, "Give me a minute to finish this prescription and we can go to my office."

I tidied up and excused myself from the backend and told Art/Gill to follow me. I closed the door and offered him a chair.

"Okay, what is this all about? Is it a coincidence that a federal agent just happened to be seated next to me on an overseas flight and now you turn up in Anniston?"

"Not a coincidence at all, Right. In fact, we've been monitoring your overseas travels since that first flight in 1976. We know you smuggled Bibles into Communist countries and were part of a crew that smuggled one million Bibles into China in 1981."

I felt the blood drain from my face. Gill was focused on my international travel, and the only Federal agency that had jurisdiction over an American citizen's international activity was the CIA. That must be the agency Gill worked for. My secret life wasn't as secret as I had thought, but why on earth was the CIA interested in my Bible smuggling? I tried to quiet the turmoil in my head and focus on what Gill was saying.

"We have a mutual friend, in fact we have three mutual friends, and it was on their recommendation that you've been on my radar since you boarded that Helsinki flight. They assured me you were made of the right stuff," he said as he chuckled at his own pun, "And, indeed, for an amateur you showed some skills at operating covertly. I'm here today to ask you to use those skills for your country."

Flummoxed, I struggled to find words. "Who are our mutual friends, and what the hell are you talking about?"

"George Daniel and I shared the same employer while he was still in the game and JB, Selma and I got acquainted when we worked together in Rhodesia."

Still at a loss for words, I muttered, "They never said anything about working with the CIA."

"Right, don't take that personally, they couldn't say anything. Everything we did was classified at one level or another. Just know that your friends think highly of you and feel you'd be able to help us out with an ongoing project."

"Uh-huh," was the best I could do.

"What we discuss today can't be taken out of this room. You can tell any curious employees that I am from the DEA checking on your records of sales of narcotic drugs."

Ignoring my blank stare and another, "Uh-huh", he continued.

"Right, I'll get to the point. Would you be willing to take an all-expense paid vacation to Russia and smuggle something out of the country rather than in?"

Since I still had no reply, he continued, "Unlike your work for Open Doors, you will be well compensated for this work."

Finally, my synapses seemed to kick back in, and I asked, "Can you give me more details?"

"You and Sue will be contract agents with the full backing of the Federal government. Your cover will be as employees of *International Travel* magazine, a company with headquarters in Falls Church, Virginia."

"Woah, wait a minute. Sue wasn't involved with my previous work with Open Door. I'm not putting her in any danger, and I'm not agreeing to anything right now, so maybe you want to be careful of what you're telling me."

"Let me finish, Right. And then, if you say no, I'll just have to kill you."

I chuckled. "Well, that sounds familiar. Is that your go-to, secret agent punch line?"

"You and Sue will take trips with different tour companies and author articles under the byline "Traveling with the Talberts". Your first trip will be to Russia the last week of October. Before that you'll fly up to Falls Church and meet the magazine staff and then join an Intourist tour group in New York. You'll fly with the group to Moscow where you'll change planes and fly to Leningrad. You'll tour Leningrad for four days then fly back to Moscow where you'll tour for three days. Sometime during these tours, a

Russian will contact you and pass you a document which you will bring back with you and give to the "editor" of the magazine. Any questions so far?"

"Yes. Do JB and George know about this?"

"No, Right. There's no reason for them to know anything about this operation. Whether you decide to tell them that you met me is totally up to you, but you can never reveal what it is you are doing for the Agency. Believe me, they know how this works. They'll never ask."

"What about Sue? She'll never be okay with playing secret agent in Russia."

"If you agree to join us, when you get home tonight tell Sue that several months ago you read an article in *International Travel* magazine advertising for travelers to take all-expense paid tours in exchange for writing articles about their travel. Tell her that it sounded like fun and on a lark you applied and today you got a phone call from the magazine wanting to interview both of you for the position. Act excited. Any other questions?"

"No, I just need this all to sink in and talk to Sue."

"Sounds good. Here's my contact number. It's the number in Virigina. Leave a message and I'll call you right back. I hope you'll decide to come on board. I'll stay in town for a couple of days. Let me know one way or another. If Sue agrees to meet, we'll set up a time."

As I watched him walk out the door and get into a rental car, I wondered how my life had just changed. That night over dinner I told Sue about reading the article in *International Travel* magazine just like Gill had outlined.

"You didn't think of mentioning something like this to me?" Sue asked. She sounded skeptical, and rightly so.

"I didn't expect to hear anything from them. I did it on a whim, but wouldn't it be fun? And if they publish the article, we get paid. All expenses are covered. HAT's traveling with the team and my staff can handle the pharmacy. You can take yourself out of the rotation at the hospital. Now that they've called me, I think it's sounds like a wonderful experience. The Assistant Editor can be in town to interview us as soon as we give them the word. If we're interested, I have a number to call so they can arrange to fly down. What do you think?"

"It's an attractive idea to travel for free and get paid, but it sounds too good to be true. I suppose it doesn't hurt to listen to what they have to say. Call them."

While Sue was washing up after dinner I made the call to Gill from my home office. As instructed, I left a message that we would like to meet with the Assistant Editor.

The next morning Gill called and said he would meet with us at 7 PM at the Victoria for dinner. I called Sue with the information. "The least we get is a free dinner at a nice restaurant. What have we got to lose? By the way, I caught the box scores in the *Post Herald* this morning. HAT won another game."

The Victoria restaurant had been a stately home sitting on the top of a hill surrounded by beautiful gardens. When the owners died, the property was sold, and the house was converted into an upscale eatery. Sue and I walked into the waiting area right on time and Gill was waiting for us. I did my best to act like I'd never seen him before.

"Would you be the Talberts?" he asked, "I'm Art Nathanson, Associate Editor of *International Travel* magazine.

He was much better at this than I. Until he introduced himself, I had not realized his real name would never be divulged.

I shook his offered hand. "Yes, we are. It's nice to meet you. This is my wife, Sue."

"Glad to meet you both. Shall we be seated? Our table is waiting for us. I hope this restaurant is satisfactory. I told my assistant to make reservations in the best restaurant in Anniston."

Over dinner, Gill really sold the subterfuge. "There were thousands of entries, more than we expected, so rather than screen each of the entries they were placed in a box and our Managing Editor reached in and pulled one out. Obviously, it was yours! Congratulations."

Sue was hanging on every word. "So, Mr. Nathanson, can you tell me how this would work; if we agreed to participate, that is."

"Of course. If you agree, we fly you up to Falls Church, Virginia where you will meet the magazine staff. After a short orientation, you'll join an Intourist tour flying out of New York. The first excursion we have planned will take you to Russia. Normally we would send a travel writer on the tour, but the editor wants to get a real traveler's perspective."

"I don't mean to sound ignorant, but what is an Intourist tour?" Sue asked.

"Intourist is the government owned tour company of Russia. Anyone who wants to tour Russia must book tours through Intourist. With everything happening in Russia right now, many people are interested in traveling there. That's why we want to do a story on travel to Russia. Did I mention that all your expenses will be paid, and you'll get $5,000 when your article is published? Your piece would be published under the byline 'Travelling with the Talberts'.

Still looking skeptical, Sue asked, "It sounds very enticing. Is it safe?"

"Absolutely safe. Hundreds, if not thousands, of Americans have toured Russia with Intourist and there's never been an incident."

"When would we be taking this tour?"

"You would arrive in Falls Church on the morning of October 30th, and you join the Intourist tour in New York on November 1st. We make all the flight arrangements. You would be back in Falls Church November 10th and give us some preliminary notes about your trip. We'll give you some guidance and any help you need to write your article which will be due the Monday after Thanksgiving. You'd be back in Anniston on the 13th. All the domestic travel would be on our corporate jet, so the accommodations will be first class."

"G.., ah Art, can you give us the evening to decide?" I said, kicking myself for almost flubbing Gill's cover.

To my surprise, Sue responded enthusiastically, "I don't know about you, Right, but I'm ready to sign. Let's do Traveling with the Talberts!"

"What do you say, Mr. Talbert? I forgot to ask, do you have passports, and do they have six months left before they expire?"

Sue looked at me thoughtfully, "We haven't used our passports since we came back from Japan in 1969. I'm sure they have expired by now."

"I did missions for Open Doors so mine may still be valid." I interjected.

"No problem, you can have passport pictures taken in the morning. Drop them off at my hotel with your old passports and we can expedite the processing and have new passports for you by the end of the week. You can pick them up when you fly up to Falls Church."

"Sue, come by the pharmacy before you go to work in the morning, and we can have pictures taken. Art, I'll have everything at your hotel before 9:00 if that works with your schedule. Now, what do we need to sign?"

Sue had no idea that she had just agreed to work covertly for the CIA, and I felt tremendously guilty keeping something so important from her, but the less she knew about the real reason behind "Traveling with the Talberts", the safer she would be.

HAT finished with an 18–2 record and was runner up to Sandy Alomar, Jr. for Rookie of the Year in the American League. HAT pitched his last game of the season on October 19th. He cleaned out his locker, loaded up the '52 Ford pickup and headed south on I-75.

Saturday afternoon on the 20th he drove down highway 431 towards Anniston. The mountains around Anniston were bursting with the fall colors. The air had a hint of the cold that winter would bring. Before driving to our house, he stopped at Couch's Jewelry Store where I always bought his mother's jewelry. HAT had gone to high school with the owner's son.

"Welcome home, HAT. Congratulations on a spectacular rookie season. How can I help you today?" Mr. Couch asked.

"I want to look at engagement rings."

"Who's the lucky lady? It wouldn't be a certain schoolteacher that the rumor mill says spent her summer in Detroit, would it?"

"That's the one. I hope she says yes when I ask her but if she doesn't, can I bring the ring back and get a refund?"

"I don't think you have to worry about her saying no, but you might have a problem with her parents. Rumor has it they aren't happy she spent the summer with you in Detroit."

"Don't know about that, Mr. Couch, but Stephanie's a grown woman."

"You know small town women love to spread rumors. I have it on good authority that the Stevens' house maid told another house maid that Stephanie had gone to Detroit for the summer. The rumor mill put two and two together and had you two living in sin to the embarrassment of the whole town. It's a good thing you are buying an engagement ring, or you might get run out of town on a rail."

"Wow, you'd never know it was 1990 here in Anniston."

Laughing, he led HAT to a glimmering showcase toward the rear of the store. "Let me show you our assortment of diamonds. I can make you a good deal on this two-carat solitaire. Do you know what size ring she wears?"

"I like the ring, but I have no idea what size she wears."

"Don't worry about it, we can size it for her later."

With the two-carat diamond ring in his pocket, HAT drove up to Hillyer High Road and rang the doorbell of the Stevens' house. When Mr. Stevens answered the door, HAT asked if he could see Stephanie.

"I'm sorry son, but Stephanie is not home right now. I think she is on a date, and I don't expect her back until late, but I will tell her that you came by."

Suddenly, the engagement ring in his pocket felt like it was burning a hole in his leg. He mumbled thank you and walked back to his truck. He drove down the mountain to our house in Golden Springs.

CHAPTER 13

Sue welcomed HAT home with his favorite meal, and we shared a couple of beers on the back deck watching a glorious sunset bathe the fall-colored leaves in a golden glow. I could tell there was a lot on HAT's mind but waited for him to feel like talking.

"Dad, being in the running for rookie of the year should help me get a big raise in my next contract."

"That's more than likely, son."

"The Kilgore Sports Agents group contacted me and guaranteed me they could get me top dollar and big endorsement deals. I think I'm going to sign with them. If I do, they said they have me lined up to be the next Aqua Velva man. That means six figures a year for basically doing nothing but smiling."

"Well HAT, I think it's a good idea to get some professional advice and management on your team."

"They also recommended that I set up residence in Florida because it has no state income tax. I'm going to look for a house in Lakeland where I have spring training and can use the Tiger Town complex to work out in during the off season. A lot of the players have houses there on a golf course where they play in the winter. I don't play golf, but I love to fish so I'm thinking about a house on a lake. Maybe when y'all retire you might move down to Lakeland where it's warm in the winter."

Sue and I had been empty nesting since HAT was out of high school, but this was his first permanent move away from us and I felt sad. I didn't want my mood to affect an enjoyable evening with my son.

"I think that's a perfect plan for your future, maybe even for your mom and I. HAT, I'm proud of you." We clinked mugs in a toast as Sue joined us.

"Your mom and I have a surprise. We've been hired by *International Travel* magazine to take all-expense paid tours and write articles about our experiences that will be published under the byline "Traveling with the Talberts.""

"Wow, Dad. That's very cool. Y'all are going to be famous writers!"

"Don't know about famous, but we get paid $5,000 for each article. We'll fly to Falls Church, Virginia on the 30th for a two-day orientation then fly out of New York on the 1st of November for a nine-day tour of Russia. We'll get back home on the 13th."

"Honey, you left out the part about flying in a private jet to and from Falls Church."

Sunday morning the phone ringing woke HAT from a deep sleep. His parents had left for Sunday school and wouldn't be back until after church. He dragged himself out of bed and walked down the hall to answer the phone.

"Hello," he croaked.

"Hi baby. Dad said you came by yesterday afternoon. I would've called last night but I didn't get back from Birmingham until late."

"Yeah, Birmingham, huh? Did you have a good time on your date?"

"Date? What date? One of the teachers from school is getting married. I went with her to help her pick out a wedding dress. I didn't expect you home until later today."

"Your dad said he thought you had a date."

"HAT, you know better than that! Do I hear a little jealousy in your voice?" Stephanie teased. "It's no secret Dad's not happy that we've been seeing each other. He almost disowned me for spending the summer with you in Detroit. He said that ball players have women in every town and that you are just playing with my affections. He wants me to date someone with a 'more stable career'."

"A stable career? What I'm doing may not be as stable as an accountant, but I'll be hiring a couple of them when my next contract's signed. We'll see how your dad feels then."

Stephanie laughed, "When can I see you?"

"I just got out of bed. Mom and Dad have gone to church. I was tired from the drive, so they let me sleep in. Give me a few minutes to get a shower and get dressed and then we can go get breakfast."

"Why don't I come over and join you in bed and you can play with my affections. Then we can take a shower together and go out for lunch."

On the 30th, Sue and I were at Anniston Municipal Airport ten minutes early for the 8 AM arrival of the private jet that would fly us to Ronald Reagan National Airport. The Cessna Citation arrived right on time, and we were in the air heading towards Washington D.C. in less than five minutes. In one hour and thirty minutes the plane was on final approach for runway 4/22 at Reagan National. The plane landed and taxied to the general aviation area where a limo was waiting and whisked us away for the short drive to the headquarters of *International Travel* magazine in Falls Church.

We were met by Art/Gill who introduced us to the Managing Editor, Raphael Abromavitz. From all appearances *International Travel* appeared to be a legitimate magazine publishing company. I realized its writers were actual travel journalists but knew that a few CIA operatives were sprinkled among the staff. It boasted offices in Paris, London, Rome, Athens, and Tokyo, all cities that would be friendly as fronts for CIA operations.

Our two-day orientation included a list of places the "Editor" wanted us to visit in each city during the tour, all with the approval of the magazine's Intourist liaison, and how to keep a log of our travels. We flew up to New York on the Delta shuttle to join our Intourist tour.

International Terminal 3 was on the other side of the airport from where the shuttle parked which meant we had an eight-minute ride on the AirTrain if you didn't count the fifteen-minute wait for the train to arrive. We squeezed in on the packed AirTrain standing up holding on to a strap. Traveling light, with only carry-ons and backpacks, we were glad we didn't have to manhandle big bags on and off the train.

At the Aeroflot desk, agents checked our passports to ensure we had visas issued by the Russian Embassy and the clerk directed us to the boarding gate. At the gate, we were met by a young lady with a sign reading "Intourist Check-in". Her name tag identified her as Sofiya, but she didn't introduce herself. A stereotypical Russian woman with a round figure, her hair was pulled back tightly into a short ponytail. She wore no makeup, a brown dress that hung on her like a sack, and shoes that resembled men's work shoes. Sofyia didn't smile. She was all business as our names were checked off the list, and we were handed name tags which she told us to wear at all times. Pointing to the waiting area, Sofyia told us to take a seat until we were called to board the plane which would be delayed by 45 minutes. Sue and I settled in to wait.

I approached a gentleman and gestured to the seats next to him, "Excuse me, are these two seats taken?" I asked.

"No, have a seat," he answered. "I see by your name tags you are on the Intourist tour with us. My name is Peter Ivanov, and this is my wife, Sara."

We exchanged pleasantries. "Glad to meet you. I'm Robert Talbert and this is my wife, Sue."

"Where are you from?" Sue asked Sara.

"Would you believe it if I told you we are from Moscow, Idaho? Well, we are. Peter's family immigrated to the United States from Russia in 1918 after the communist revolution in 1917. He is the fire chief in Moscow, and I am the secretary for the mayor. Where are you folks from?"

Peter looked like he might be 6'6" and was all muscle. I estimated that they were in their early '40s. He would be a good friend to have if you ever got into a fight.

"We're from Anniston, Alabama," Sue answered.

"What line of work are you in Robert?" Peter asked.

"I am a pharmacist and Sue is a nurse."

For the next hour and a half, Peter talked constantly. He had played football at Washington State and had a tryout with the Raiders. I mostly just sat there and nodded as he dominated the conversation.

When the announcement was made to board the plane, the Intourist group were allowed to board first. The Russian IL-86 aircraft had a twin-isle interior with nine-abreast seating in a 3-3-3 layout. Three rows were marked off for our group and we could sit in any seat on the three rows. Peter sat down in an aisle seat and his wife sat across the aisle from him. Sue sat next to his wife, and I got an aisle seat. Thank goodness, I was far enough away from Peter that I would not have to listen to him talk for the next nine hours.

The flight attendant in our section looked like she was a refugee from the Soviet men's hockey team. She never smiled, so I couldn't see if she was missing her front teeth. After the safety announcements, which were in Russian, we got an announcement which was also in Russian. I assumed it was the pilot welcoming us and telling us about the flight to Moscow, but I wasn't sure. With the Soviet Union in near collapse, I worried about the maintenance of the plane.

I crossed my fingers and said a silent prayer as the plane raced down the runway. We were soon climbing towards our cruising altitude. I found myself listening to determine if the engines were running smoothly. After about an hour I was satisfied that maybe we would make it to Moscow. I dozed off but I woke up thinking I heard a strange noise. I listened to make sure the engines were still running, and they were. I could hear Peter talking to the person sitting next to him. I don't think he was quiet for more than twenty minutes the whole flight. About an hour before our scheduled landing the hockey player came by with breakfast. A hard roll, something that resembled meat and hot tea. I asked if I could get coffee.

"No coffee, tea!" she barked.

"Do you have cream and sugar?"

"No!"

This was a forewarning of what was to come in the food department during our trip. Sue made notes in the journal she purchased to record impressions of our tour. We landed at Puskin International Airport at 1300 hours and had a two-and-a-half-hour layover before our flight to Leningrad. The USSR used military time. It brought back memories of when I was in the Air Force. We went through immigration and were herded into an area for foreign tourists. The area used by Russian travelers was off limits to our group. As I was walking to a seat to wait for the next flight, I heard Peter talking to our tour guide. They were carrying on a conversation in Russian. Sue and I found two seats together. Sara came and sat down next to Sue.

"Peter is practicing his Russian. His family still speaks Russian when they don't want me to know what they are talking about. It used to bother me, but now I just ignore them."

When our flight was called for Leningrad, my stomach was telling me it was time to give it some food. That mystery meat, hard roll and hot tea had long ago been digested and my stomach was growling. It would growl a lot on this trip. Our plane for this leg of our trip was the IL-18 turboprop which Aeroflot had set up for 80 passengers. We didn't have any reserved seats so we had to take what we could find. Luckily, we found two seats together.

My worries about aircraft maintenance came back with a vengeance when the pilot started the engines and they backfired and then ran rough for two minutes before they began to run smoothly. I crossed my fingers, said my prayer and it must have worked because we were soon headed down the runway and lifting off the ground.

In about two hours we landed at Pulkovo International Airport. As we walked into the terminal, Sofiya was holding an Intourist flag. We followed her to the baggage area where, by some miracle, everyone's luggage had made it from New York. After retrieving their bags, our group followed Sofiya out to a bus that looked like it was on its last legs. A trail of black diesel smoke followed us the entire 23 KM to our hotel.

CHAPTER 14

Like our bus, the hotel had seen better days. You could tell that at one time it had been grand, but years of communist neglect had taken its toll. After giving out room keys, Sofiya announced that dinner would be served at 5:30 in the main dining room. People were grumbling about the use of military time so Sofiya, sensing her group would never be on time, resorted to the familiar standard time. I wondered what those folks would do when she refused to forego metric in favor of imperial measurements for distance.

The elevator that took us up to the third floor was something out of the ancient past. The operator looked at our keys, nodded and closed the door, and put the elevator in motion. It made a strange noise as it struggled to lift us to the third floor. We were met by the "Hall Witch" as we exited the elevator who inspected our room key and entered it into her register. We were then permitted to go to our room.

The room was very spacious, but the furniture appeared as if it hadn't been updated since 1917. The small TV with rabbit ears sat on a table across the room from a large, overstuffed chair. I noticed right away that there was no water closet or a clothes closet. We found the communal bath at the end of the hall. There was a ceramic chamber pot under the bed for late night emergencies. Sue made copious notes in her journal.

Sue felt like a short walk before dinner to stretch our legs after all the sitting on the plane. When we got to the elevator the Hall Witch stopped us and took our key. She then made a notation in her register, gave us back our key, and allowed us to get on the elevator when it arrived.

It was cold and spitting snow as we walked along the street. It was starting to get dark, so we didn't walk very far before we turned around and headed back to the hotel. Our group was already in the dining room when we arrived. As we walked in, Peter stood up and waved us over to where he had saved us two seats next to them.

"How is your room? Do you have a bathroom?" Sara asked.

"Yes, we have a bathroom, but it's down at the end of the hall. We have a chamber pot under the bed for late night emergencies," Sue chuckled.

"I'll have to look when we go up. We didn't look under the bed!"

Peter chimed in, "Our TV picks up one station. I watched the local news before we came down. There is a hockey game on tonight. I am going to watch it if I can stay awake. Do you like hockey?"

"Never watched hockey," I replied, "We're big baseball fans. Our son Herbert pitches for the Detroit Tigers. He is in the running for rookie of the year in the American League."

"Get out of here!" Peter exclaimed, "HAT is your son? We were at a fire chief's conference in Seattle this summer and watched him pitch a four hitter. I know you two must be immensely proud of him."

Before Peter could say anything else our dinner arrived. Mystery meat, cabbage, potatoes, a colorless soup, and a piece of brown bread with the texture of sawdust served with hot tea, no cream, no sugar.

After dinner, Sofiya announced that breakfast would be at 0700 hours. It appeared she assumed the ignorant foreigners could convert anything prior to 1200 hours easily.

"Don't be late or you will have nothing to eat. Our tour starts promptly at 0745 hours. If you have not given your passports to the desk, do so before retiring for the evening. The government official will come by to check them against the tour roster. If you have not turned in your passport you can be fined a large amount and possibly go to jail."

Sue and I stayed in the lobby after dinner and met some of our fellow travelers. Most of them were world travelers. Sue and Sara found two women who played bridge. Sue always carried a deck of cards in her purse, so they got a game going. They soon had a group of spectators wanting to challenge the winners.

Not being a card player, I wandered into the bar with Peter and ordered a beer. The bartender drew two Stepan Razin drafts. There was a small black and white TV behind the bar. In Russian Peter asked the bartender if he would turn on the hockey game. This led to a long harangue by the bartender. Peter explained that if the bartender turned on the TV, he would have to charge us an entertainment tax. It would cost us one ruble each to watch the game. Peter said he thought the bartender had his own side hustle going without the hotel approval. I paid the two rubles. I would add it to my expense account when I got back to Falls Church.

Soon a second bridge game got organized and most of the men had gathered in the bar. Peter explained to the new arrivals that an entertainment tax of one ruble would be added to their bills because of the TV. As the group expanded the bartender announced that everyone must buy something from the bar and pay the entertainment tax or leave. I sang the praises of the beer and said it was a bargain even with the entertainment tax. Beer would turn out to be my main nourishment on this tour. A couple of guys got up and left but most stayed and ordered Razin drafts. Peter translated the announcer's call of the game and everyone in the bar got into the game, even me. The game ended at about 2100 hours and the card games were breaking up, so we decided to call it a night. I knew after drinking two drafts that I would be using the chamber pot during the night.

Sue and I woke early the next morning and took cold showers. Before heading down for breakfast, Sue made notes in her journal. In the dining room, Sofiya had on the same clothes she was wearing when we met her in New York. Breakfast was one boiled egg, a hard roll, a small piece of cheese and hot tea, no cream, no sugar. After breakfast, we followed Sofiya and the Intourist flag out to the old smoke-belching bus. Sofiya informed us we were going to be the first tour group of the morning to visit the State Hermitage Museum.

As we drove, Sofiya informed us the museum was founded in 1762 when Catherine the Great acquired an extensive collection of paintings from John Ernst Gotzkowsky. According to Sofiya the museum now holds the largest collection of paintings in the world and is spread across six buildings. Explaining there was no way we could see all the paintings she assured us she would lead us to the most famous artists' works. I am not a fan of art galleries, so I wasn't looking forward to the next two hours.

After thirty minutes of listening to Sofiya talk about paintings, I told Sue I would meet her at the gift shop. On my way a Russian man approached me and asked if I was an American. He spoke particularly good English. I told him that yes, I was an American, and he said he had something he would like to discuss with me in private. I thought this could be my contact, so I followed him back down the hall. He stopped in front of a large painting.

"Do you like art?" he asked.

"It's not really my thing, but my wife likes to visit art galleries, so I come along while she enjoys the paintings," I replied.

"Does she like ballet?"

"Yes, she does."

"They are performing Swan Lake at the Kirov Ballet tonight and I can sell you two tickets for $10 American. They are exceptionally good seats. My wife and I can't go so I need to get my money back for the tickets. Would you be interested?"

Caught off guard by his offer, I explained that I'd have to check with my wife first. "You stay right here, and I will run and ask her."

Clearly uncomfortable with my suggestion he said, "I can't stay in one place too long because security will get suspicious. It's against the law to resell tickets. I will wait in the next gallery. Don't take long."

I rushed back to where the group was and asked Sue if she would like to go see Swan Lake at the Kirov Ballet. "I can get two tickets for tonight's performance for $10."

"Where can you get tickets?" she asked, unsure about this new addition to our itinerary.

"I just met a Russian man on my way to the gift shop who has two tickets he can't use and wants to get his money back."

"What if they are counterfeit?" she asked, always skeptical about good things that drop out of the sky.

"I don't think a crime syndicate counterfeits ballet tickets, especially here in Russia," I offered.

Sara overheard our discussion about the tickets and said that she and Peter would love to go if we passed.

"I don't believe his story," Peter stated emphatically, "I think he is a scalper. He waits around here and sells tickets to tourists. I bet if I ask, he can sell us more tickets. Ask the group if they would like to go to the ballet tonight rather than play cards in the lobby," he suggested.

I went around to the group and told them about the ballet. Everyone wanted to go and were willing to pay $5.00 per ticket. Sofiya came up to me and told me that the tickets were from black marketeers, and we should not buy them. "He buys the tickets very cheaply and then sells them to tourists."

"Would you like to see Swan Lake? I'll buy you a ticket," I offered. Not surprisingly, Sofiya declined.

I headed back to meet the ticket scalper and found him admiring a painting.

I stood beside him and said, "I need 19 tickets. I'll pay $5 U.S."

"I don't have 19 tickets, but I can get them by this afternoon. Where are you staying?" he said.

"The Grand Hotel European."

"Here are two tickets, give me $10. Be outside of the hotel at 1600 hours. I will bring the rest of the tickets; you bring the money. Be on time because I can't wait for you because of security. I will be in a taxi."

After two hours gazing at paintings, I was ready to get back on the bus. As we approached the bus, we were swarmed by young people selling T-shirts, real fur Russian hats, sweatshirts emblazoned with "Hermitage Museum", and Russian watches in military time. My ears were getting cold, so I decided to buy a hat. After a little haggling, I paid $10. Once the boys saw me buy the hat, it was like chum in the water, and they were sharks. Sofiya came along and shooed them away so we could get on the bus.

As we drove away, one of the tour members said they had bought a sweatshirt, but the seller didn't have the correct change. The seller told him that he would get change and meet the bus at our next stop. I heard the man's wife tell him he would never see his change. I agreed with her.

Our next stop was the Battleship Aurora which had fired the first shot in the Russian Revolution in 1917. As the bus pulled into the parking lot next to the ship, there stood the sweatshirt salesman waving, along with the other young entrepreneurs. Because of his honesty, he sold five more sweatshirts. Sofiya, in tour-guide mode, proceeded to tell us about the ship's importance in Russian history and suggested everyone snap pictures. Soon we were back on the bus spreading pollution on the way to Kazan Cathedral. The young entrepreneurs were following us on their motorbikes.

I was astonished by the beautiful churches in this atheist country. I asked Sofiya if the people still practiced Christianity. Of course, I knew the answer because I had smuggled Bibles into Russia, but I wanted to see if a government employee would give an honest answer. Sofiya explained that the cathedrals were no longer used for churches since religion was not recognized by the government.

"They are now museums, enjoyed for their beautiful architecture." As the group took pictures, Sofiya came and stood beside me and whispered, "Those of us who are believers hold church in our homes. We must be careful not to draw attention to our meetings."

Our next stop was the hotel for lunch. More mystery meat, which Peter called the roadkill of the day, more cabbage, potatoes, watery soup, sawdust bread, hot tea, no sugar, no cream. Something new had been added to the menu, a pad of butter. Sue took notes.

The afternoon was free for us to sightsee on our own. Sofiya warned us about going into a Russian cafe or taking pictures of people waiting in line to buy food. She said either one could get us arrested.

Sue, Sara, and Peter wanted to spend more time at the Hermitage to see galleries that they missed during our visit. As we walked, we passed men in ragged military uniforms who were begging. Some were missing a limb, others looked as if they might be blind. They all looked as if they were half starved. I assumed they were veterans of Russia's war in Afghanistan which had ended in 1989 when Russia withdrew after years of stalemate.

The walk in the cold made me thankful that I had bought a fur hat. When we got to the Hermitage, I found a bench near the gift shop and sat down.

"I'll be here when you finish," I told them, "Remember I meet the scalper at 4:00 at the hotel."

CHAPTER 15

I thought Peter's Russian and being an imposing big man might come in handy when I met the scalper, so I asked him to go with me. Promptly at 1600 hours a taxi pulled up to the front of the hotel and my scalper friend was sitting in the front seat next to the driver. The driver looked like someone you wouldn't want to meet in a dark alley. He had long greasy hair and what looked like four days of beard growth.

"Get in. We can't transact business here," the scalper ordered.

Peter got in behind the driver and I got in behind our scalper. As soon as the doors were closed the cab took off down the street. He made a right turn at the first intersection, went two blocks, made a U-turn, and then a right turn into an alley. We went down the alley until the cab was unseen from the street. The driver stopped. The thought that we might have made a big mistake crossed my mind. This could be the place where they pulled a gun and robbed us.

"You got the money?" the scalper asked.

"Do you have the tickets?" I replied.

He held up seventeen tickets.

"I have four front-row orchestra seats and the other 13 are spread out on the main floor."

He handed me the tickets and I handed him the money.

"I bought you and your wife souvenir programs. You will want to keep them to remember the evening so don't lose them. It's been nice doing business with you."

He reached over and gave me the programs and I noticed him smile. I was sure he was happy making such a big sale. He then said something to the driver and got out of the taxi. He walked a little way down the alley, opened a door and went inside. I looked over at Peter and asked what he had said to the driver.

"He said to take us back to the hotel and he would see the driver at home tonight."

When we arrived back at the hotel, Sofiya offered to get the bus to take us to the ballet and the driver agreed to charge each of us less than the cost of a cab ride. I was sure that he would kick some of the money back to Sofiya and give some to his dispatcher.

Everyone had a great evening. When the show was over, in Russian, Peter asked if we could get autographs of the dancers. The lead ballerina wanted to know if we were Americans and Peter told her yes. She explained they were going to tour North American in the spring and asked him if we would give her our addresses in America. She said that she wanted to practice writing in English and boasted that she had pen pals from all over the world.

Peter wondered, "Doesn't the government security read your mail to and from foreign countries?"

She lowered her voice and answered, "Yes, they do, but it's fun to give them something to keep them busy. Maybe I will see you when I come to America."

The next morning, we got another surprise at breakfast. There was cream and sugar for our tea! Sue made notes as Sofiya explained that there would only be one dairy serving per day. Our first morning tour was to the Church of the Savior on the Spilled Blood. It was built on the site where Alexander II was fatally wounded in the assassination attempt on March 1, 1881. The official name of the church is Church of the Resurrection of Jesus Christ, but the locals have always called it Church of the Savior on the Spilled Blood.

Our second stop for the morning was the Leningrad in the WWII Exposition which is housed in the Count Nikolay Rumyantsev's mansion overlooking the Neva River. Loving

WWII history, this was my kind of museum. The building is beautiful so if you appreciate architecture, it is worth the visit just for that, but it also told the story of the 900-day siege of Leningrad during WWII. During the siege, 800,000 citizens died from starvation, exposure, disease, and shelling from distant German artillery. It was one of the most grueling and memorable sieges in history. Painted canvases of starving people are displayed on the walls.

After seeing the disturbing scenes, I was overcome with the strength of the human spirit. Many Americans don't grasp the horrors of WWII. The Russian people and the Jews of Europe know firsthand the inhuman treatment that came from Nazi Germany and Adolph Hitler.

Our next stop was the Piskaryovskoye Memorial Cemetery where nearly a half a million civilians who died in the siege are buried in mass graves. There is an eternal flame, a statue of the Motherland, and photographs and documents describing the siege. As we rode back to the hotel, I felt ashamed that I had complained about the food we were being served. Our meals were a feast compared to what the people of Leningrad had to eat during the siege.

After the noon meal, we were on our own for the afternoon. I checked the list of places our editor at *International Travel* wanted us to visit and decided on a walk to the Neva River. I had observed the large navy ships when we came by on our way to the hotel.

Sue and Sara found two ladies who wanted to play bridge, so Peter and I were on our own. As we approached a battlecruiser and destroyer, a large group of Russian sailors walked towards us. One of the sailors asked in broken English if we had any spare cigarettes. Peter answered him in Russian which seemed to upset the sailor who looked startled and seemed apprehensive. Peter spoke again, and the sailors smiled. Peter unzipped his backpack and took out a carton of Marlboros. Peter said something else, and the sailor took off his watch and his uniform cap and gave them to Peter in exchange for four packs of Marlboros. Peter turned to me and said, "The watch cost three packs and the cap was one pack. Would you like a cap as a souvenir?"

"Sure, I'd like an officer's cap," I replied, enjoying the display of bartering I was witnessing.

Peter told the sailor what I had said, and the sailor said he would go back to the ship and get me one, but it would cost three packs.

"Tell him I will give two packs," I insisted, assuming no first offer was the last.

Peter translated my offer and the young sailor turned and ran back to the ship. We waited a few minutes for him to return with what looked like a laundry bag. When he opened the bag there were four caps like he had sold Peter and one officer's cap. There would be some angry sailors on board when they found out that their caps had been stolen.

At dinner we had the roadkill of the day, cabbage, potatoes, sawdust bread, hot tea, no sugar, no cream.

On the advice of a friend, I had brought two rolls of toilet paper with me. It was wise advice because you could see the wood in the Russian toilet paper. I decided that the people in Russia didn't smile because they all had hemorrhoids from using the terrible toilet paper. In a war with NATO, the Russian commanders would motivate their troops to fight by telling them they would get NATO's good toilet paper if they won.

Our third day began with the same breakfast we had the previous two mornings. We followed the Intourist flag out to the smog-belching bus, and we were off to visit the Peter and Paul Fortress. At every site there was always a group of young men selling souvenirs. The capitalist, entrepreneurial spirit was alive in this Communist country.

The Peter and Paul Cathedral inside the fortress was the first and oldest landmark in Leningrad. It was built between 1712 and 1733 on Hare Island along the Neva River. It contained the remains of almost all the Russian emperors and empresses. An artist outside the cathedral had pictures of Leningrad for sale and Sue bought her first souvenir, a beautiful painting of the cathedral. The artist rolled it up and placed it in a small cardboard tube so it would not get damaged. I noticed Sofiya walk over and say something to the artist. The artist handed her something. I assumed that it was her kickback.

Our next stop was the Military Historical Museum of Artillery, Engineers and Signal Corps which is housed in a crownwork of the Fortress. There were exhibits of weapons from the 18th century up to modern times. I found it interesting that there was a room dedicated to the Kalashnikov AK-47 and its designer, Mikhail Kalashnikov. Sue and Sara grew impatient having to wait as Peter and I read about the different weapons and decided to wait outside in the fresh air. They were joined by a rather large group of wives who also didn't have any interest in weapons.

When Peter and I were back out on the street, I was approached by a young man selling watches.

"Excuse me sir, do you have a few minutes to help me with my conversational English?" he asked politely.

I was startled by the unusual request. "I guess, we have five more minutes before we leave."

"Where in America are you from?" he asked.

"I'm from Alabama," I answered.

"War Eagle, beat 'Bama!" he exclaimed to my surprise.

"How do you know about Auburn and our archrival the University of Alabama?"

"We have a radio that picks up Radio Free Europe and sometimes we get American Forces Network from Stavanger Air base in Norway. I listen for it every night. I like listening to Armed Forces Network because they broadcast in English. The late-night DJ at Stavanger is from Alabama and always ends his show with 'Until tomorrow, War Eagle, beat 'Bama'."

"My wife is waving to me, so I need to get on the bus. It has been nice talking to you. War Eagle."

"Sir, I have a small gift for you," he said, handing me a Russian military 2400-hour watch.

"I can't take that."

"It doesn't work so I can't sell it, but it will make a nice souvenir to remember me by, so please take it," he insisted.

"What is your name?" I asked.

"Mikhail Petrov."

"My name is Robert Talbert. Glad to meet you Mikhail. Thank you for the watch. When I look at it, I will think of you."

Another dinner of roadkill, cabbage, potatoes, sawdust bread, hot tea, no sugar, no cream awaited us at the hotel. Sofiya announced that we would check out of the hotel in the morning before we left for our tour of Catherine's Palace and Peterhof Grand Palace. Afterward we would go directly to the airport for our late afternoon flight to Moscow.

"Have all your belongings with you when you come down for breakfast. Your baggage will be loaded on the bus while we are having breakfast. Please settle any charges you owe the hotel tonight and they will give you your passports."

The next morning, the Hall Witch signed us out for the last time. I gave her a small tip for her diligent service during our stay. She smiled for the first time and said, "Спасибо". I slipped the elevator operator a small tip for his service, and he also smiled and said "Спасибо". The word sounded like spuh-SEE-buh, and I assumed it must mean thank you. At breakfast we got a surprise. There was a slice of awful-tasting cheese.

When we arrived at Catherine's Summer Palace, I could understand why the serfs might be upset with the Romanovs. The Grand Ballroom measures 154' by 56'. Sue and Sara had discovered their favorite place on our tour. When the German forces retreated after the siege of Leningrad during WWII, they intentionally burned the Palace leaving only a hollow shell behind. The palace reconstruction was begun in 1957 by the State Control Commission for the Preservation of Monuments and took 23 years to complete.

After touring the palace and the grounds we had a light lunch in one of the buildings by the lake. More cabbage, potatoes, and hot tea.

Our next stop was Peter's Palace which is actually a series of palaces. Peter the Great had palace envy after seeing Louis XIV's Versailles and built the Versailles of Russia. Construction began in1705 and was completed in1755. It sits on 1500 acres of formal gardens with 173 glorious fountains fed by underground springs. Much of Peter's palace was destroyed by the Germans and was restored by the same State Control Commission for Preservation of Historical Monuments. After touring the Grand Palace and some of the gardens it was back on the bus for our drive to the airport.

CHAPTER 16

As we boarded our Aeroflot IL-18 plane for our flight to Moscow, I saw something I had never seen before or since on a commercial aircraft; there was a table with two seats on each side facing each other. Sue and her bridge buddies promptly took possession of the four seats and pulled out the cards. I found a vacant window seat next to a Russian lady who appeared to be traveling alone. As the plane was climbing to its cruising altitude, the sunset gave the clouds a wondrous color. *God, you gave us a beautiful sunset today.*

I had not realized I had spoken out loud until my Russian neighbor asked in accented English, "Why do you believe in God?"

That was a question I had never been asked before, even with years of teaching Sunday school. I thought for a few moments before answering, and for the duration of the flight we talked about God. As we prepared to land, she thanked me for sharing my beliefs, explaining that priests and preachers always seemed to want something but that I had given her something, asking nothing in return. I opened my backpack and took out a small New Testament that Russian customs had allowed me to keep and gave it to her. I genuinely believe God sat me next to that woman so I could plant a seed.

On the bus from the airport to our hotel, I overheard one of my fellow travelers say that Moscow had the largest McDonalds in the world and wouldn't a Big Mac taste good tonight. That got me thinking, maybe the bus driver could take us to the McDonalds. I asked Sofiya if it was possible. She explained that the driver had to account for all his diesel fuel, and it would be impossible for him to drive to McDonalds.

"Peter, would you like a Big Mac and a chocolate shake tonight instead of mystery meat, cabbage, and potatoes? If we can persuade the bus driver to take us to McDonalds, I'll buy."

Peter walked to the front of the bus, and I could hear him speaking to the driver in Russian.

When he returned to his seat he explained, "Alexander said we would have to pay for the diesel and give him a little money for his time."

I stood up and sang, *"We deserve a break today at McDonalds"*, and explained my idea. I took off my Russian fur cap and walked up the aisle asking everyone if they would contribute to the McDonald fund. My cap was soon running over. I walked up to Alexander, showed him the money, and he nodded yes.

He told Peter that when we got to the hotel to drop off our luggage we must come right back to the bus because he couldn't stay parked long or security would start asking questions and order him to leave. When the bus stopped everyone rushed inside the hotel with their luggage, dropped it off, and returned to the bus. As Sue and I were leaving the lobby, a Russian woman approached us and asked if I was with the group that was going to McDonalds? How did she know about our clandestine adventure? Did Sofiya rat us out to security?

Before my imagination carried me away, the woman explained, "My name is Anna and I'm an Intourist guide. Sofiya told me about your trip to McDonalds, but she can't go with you because she is taking care of paperwork. If I can catch a ride with you into town, it will save me the cost of the Metro. I must meet a new group that is staying at the Intourist hotel downtown."

We were the last three on the bus and as soon as the door closed, we headed out of the parking lot. When we got to the McDonalds, there was a line four deep and a block long waiting to get in. That didn't discourage us because there was American food at the other end of the line. Anna and Alexander stayed aboard the bus and offered to wait for us while we ate.

"Have you ever had a Big Mac?" I asked.

"No, they are too expensive for most Russians. Mostly foreigners eat here," Anna explained.

"Well, tonight you are going to get your first Big Mac, a chocolate shake, french fries and a fried apple pie. Dinner is my treat."

Being the largest McDonalds in the world, the line moved quickly and in less than ten minutes I was ordering our four meals. Never had a Big Mac tasted so good. The cold chocolate shake tasted like the nectar of the gods and each fry sent waves of ecstasy crashing through my taste buds.

When we got back on the bus, I gave Alexander the money I had collected. Anna watched, amazed, as I paid him.

"You just gave him what amounts to six months wages," she explained, and I could see her entrepreneurial brain kick into gear. "Would you like a night tour of Moscow?" she asked, "We can go to Arbat Street, Red Square, St. Basil's Cathedral, the Kremlin and watch the changing of the guards at midnight at Lenin's Mausoleum."

I took off my cap and walked down the aisle. When I came back to the front of the bus my cap was full and we were off on a magical night tour. The fresh snow and the lights of the city gave the illusion of a winter wonderland. It was a night that 18 American tourists would never forget. After watching the changing of the guards at Lenin's Mausoleum at midnight, it was time to get back on the bus and go to our hotel. We were walking to the bus when Anna asked me what was on our agenda for today since it was now past midnight and the 7th of November.

"We're scheduled to go to some museum before lunch and we have the afternoon free."

"It doesn't sound like the museum tour appeals to you. Would you like to go to the military parade instead?" she asked.

"Sofiya told us that American tour groups can't attend the parade," I answered.

"They can't, but I will get you in with my group," she smiled. "You can catch the Metro Red Line at the Yugo Station just down the street from your hotel. It's a twenty-minute ride to the Okhotny Ryad Metro Station. Hotel Intourist, where my group is staying, is 100 meters to the left after you come out of the station. Take the underpass at the end of Tverskaya and I will meet you in front of the hotel at 0800. The signs in the Metro are also in English, relics of the 1980 Olympics, so it will be easy for you. Hotel Salut where your group is staying was built for the '80 Olympics but sat nearly empty because of the boycott. I'm sure Intourist put your group way out there because they want to keep you away from the parade."

"Would you write the directions down for me?" I asked.

She reached into her satchel, "Here is a Metro map. I will mark it for you."

Alexander dropped Anna off at her hotel then drove us to Hotel Salut which was miles away, near the perimeter road that encircled Moscow. It was almost 0130 hours when our clandestine adventure came to an end. Our new Hall Witch was asleep when we got off the elevator and tiptoed past her to our room. Our room was smaller than our room in Leningrad, but it had a small bath with a shower. Before turning in, Sue made her daily entries in her journal.

At breakfast, we told Sofiya we were skipping the morning tour and would sightsee on our own. I could tell she wasn't pleased with our decision, but she said nothing. We caught the Metro and were headed downtown by 0715. The Metro was different from any public transportation I had ever been on. The station was clean and had artwork on the walls. There was no graffiti anywhere. The train became more crowded the nearer we got to downtown. Families were going to the parade to take part in what would probably be the last celebration of the Revolution as the USSR empire was crumbling. I noticed a heavy police presence everywhere. There were no young people selling trinkets as there had been in Leningrad. As we exited the Metro station, we witnessed two policemen grab a young man and begin hitting him with clubs. We watched as they marched him off towards a waiting van. Police were stopping people at random asking for their identification papers. I told Sue not to make eye contact with anyone and to keep walking towards the Hotel Intourist where I could see Anna standing outside.

"Take off the name tags Sofiya gave you and put these on," she instructed us. "You are now part of my tour group. It's a group sponsored by the Communist Party of England, but I don't think there is a communist among them. They are a bunch of old union members and intellectuals from some university. Stay close to me and we should not have any problem getting you into our reserved area."

On Red Square, large banners were hung from the buildings announcing the "73rd Anniversary October Revolution". One banner was an enormous picture of Lenin, and another with only the date "1990". As it turned out, we did witness the last parade celebrating the anniversary of the start of the Communist Revolution.

We worked our way to the front of the crowd to the area that was reserved for our adopted group. I found a space where I could take pictures without being obstructed by people's heads. I had four rolls of film for my camera and would use them all before the parade was over.

The people in the crowd began to cheer when the limousine carrying the commander of the parade, Colonel General Nikolai Kulinin, entered Red Square from our left. His car was followed by military bands and seemingly endless rows of marching troops with their high-stepping gate. Then came the requisite display of the USSR's military equipment. As the last tank rumbled by, after nearly two hours, the end was in sight and the good communist citizens joined the parade.

We later learned that one of the people who joined the parade was Alexander Shmonov, an unemployed machinist from Leningrad. Alexander had been a respectable Soviet citizen who worked as an engineer in a factory and followed the Party line until President Brezhnev temporarily stopped blocking the BBC and Voice of America radio stations. While listening to their broadcasts Alexander heard the truth about what was going on in the USSR and the persecution of dissidents.

In 1989 he joined the Leningrad People's Front which demanded the democratization of the political system. He was arrested four times for passing out leaflets telling people not to vote for the communist slate of electors. In 1990, he decided the only way to bring about democracy was to assassinate President Mikhail Gorbachev. He purchased a hunting rifle, sawed off the barrel and intended to kill Gorby when he passed the reviewing stand at the parade.

When the President was within range, Shmonov took out the rifle hidden under his long coat, and took aim. However, before he could pull the trigger a police sergeant spotted him, grabbed his arm, and the shot missed Gorbachev. Alexander was arrested and charged with attempted terrorism. He was declared insane because no sane person would attempt to shoot the President. He would spend five years in the State Mental Health Hospital before he admitted what he did was wrong and asked the State to forgive him. He was finally released.

There was nothing on Russian TV, radio, or in the next day's newspapers about the attempted assassination. Sue and I would hear about it when we got back to New York.

The following day our tour group visited Red Square and the sites of Moscow during the light of day. The snow was dirty and the magic we saw on our night tour was gone, replaced with a dull gray. I noticed there were fewer police, and I didn't see any men in dark suits and black trench coats standing near the entrances to the buildings like there had been the day before. The festive atmosphere of the people was gone. They walked with heads down, not making eye contact with anyone they passed. As we started to cross the street a bus came by and began to blow its horn. It was the driver from our night tour. When we got to our next stop on the itinerary, the Bolshoi Theater, Sofiya told us that they were performing the Nutcracker. She said all performances were sold out, but Intourist had tickets for $50 if anyone was interested.

When our tour concluded I informed Sofiya that Sue and I would not return to the hotel on the bus. We wanted to do some more sightseeing on our own and would catch the Metro back to the hotel. She reminded me the group was going to the Moscow Circus and we needed to be back in time to catch the bus in 1900 hours. I explained that we had other plans and wouldn't be going to the circus. Again, I saw Sofiya wasn't comfortable with our decision, but she made no objections.

Peter and Sara decided to stay with us. We had passed a newly opened Pizza Hut during our tour. Sofiya explained it was for tourists and foreigners, again because Russians couldn't afford to eat there. I thought I remembered how to get there, and pizza sounded a lot better than another cabbage, potatoes, and mystery meat meal. I led the way, and we were soon ordering a deep pan pizza with the works and four large Pepsi's.

"I think we can buy tickets to the Bolshoi for tonight's Nutcracker performance from a scalper a lot cheaper than $50," I suggested. "I noticed some young men standing off to the side when we were there. One gave me a nod when Sofiya was talking about tickets. Would y'all be interested in going if we can get tickets at a reasonable price?"

Peter spoke up and said he wanted to go to the circus, but Sara had other ideas. "You can go to the circus; I'm going to see the Nutcracker if Robert gets us tickets." We returned to the Bolshoi and saw four young men standing a few meters from the entrance. I approached the young man who had given me the nod earlier and he asked if I was interested in tickets.

"I need four in the orchestra area."

"Don't have orchestra. Have four, front row, first balcony. Twenty dollars US each ticket."

"I'll give you ten dollars each," I countered.

"Fifteen dollars," he insisted.

"Ten dollars each and a pack of Marlboros."

"Ten dollars each, four packs and is a deal," was his final offer.

"Done."

Peter unzipped his backpack and removed four packs of Marlboros. We gave the scalper $40, and he handed us the tickets. That night, while our group was watching the Moscow Circus, we had the cultural highlight of our tour. Seeing the Nutcracker in the beautiful Bolshoi Theater was a once-in-a-lifetime experience.

Our last day in Moscow was spent visiting the Pushkin Museum and the Armory Museum. On the drive we passed a small lake which Sofiya claimed was the inspiration for the ballet Swan Lake.

After a ten-hour flight we were glad to be back on American soil. We said goodbye to Peter and Sara, promised to keep in touch and caught the flight to Washington where we were met by Gill Maxwell, aka "Art".

"How was your trip?" Art/Gill asked as he took Sue's backpack and led us to a Town Car parked at curbside. During the drive, Sue gave Art/Gill a lengthy commentary about our trip and assured him she had taken excellent notes about our impressions and experiences.

When we arrived at *International Travel* magazine Sue excused herself and headed for the restroom. Gill wasted no time in asking if a Russian had given me anything.

I thought back and said, "A ticket scalper in Leningrad gave me two programs which he said would make good souvenirs of our night at the Kirov Ballet, and a young man who was selling watches gave me a broken 24-hour watch that he said he couldn't sell."

"Give them to me," Gill said. The tone of his voice told me not to argue.

I dug into my backpack for the watch and the programs and handed them over. Gill popped open the back of the watch to reveal a single tiny piece of film.

"What the hell is that?" I asked, staring at the pieces of the watch in Gill's hand.

Smiling, now using his pleasant voice, he said, "I may be mistaken, but I believe you just smuggled out the plans for a top-secret Russian nuclear sub."

Staring at him in disbelief, I had no words.

"You can keep the watch," he offered as he handed me the pieces. "After our people go over the programs for coded messages, we'll give them back to you as well."

Our article "Mystery Meat, Cabbage and Potatoes: Our Trip to Russia" was published in the March issue of *International Traveler*.

CHAPTER 17

HAT was enjoying playing house with Stephanie while we were away. One day, HAT returned from a workout to be met by Stephanie at the front door. She had found the diamond engagement ring while doing a load of laundry and was holding it in her hand.

"When were you planning to ask me to marry you?" she asked.

HAT wasn't sure if she was happy or annoyed when he answered. "I was going to ask you the day I got home from Detroit, but you weren't home. Knowing your dad didn't approve of me, I decided to wait."

"Well, I'm here now, are you going to ask me? You know the whole town is gossiping about us living in sin. The principal at school reminded me there is a morals clause in my contract. This is the deep South, HAT, she said we are not setting the right example for my fifth graders."

HAT took her in his arms, "Will you marry me and let me make you an honest woman? I don't want you to lose your job."

Pulling away, placing a finger on her chin as if considering the offer, she teased, "Only if you get down on one knee and put the ring on my finger."

The next day Stephanie walked into her principal's office and showed off her engagement ring. Within days she moved into an apartment across the street from the school and announced that she and HAT were getting married in March in Lakeland, Florida where HAT would be for spring training with the Detroit Tigers.

Stephanie's mother, Harriet, didn't like the idea of a wedding in Lakeland, preferring a big wedding in June at Saint Michael's All Angels Episcopal Church with the reception at the country club. That would be more in tune with their social status in Anniston.

Stevens Foundry had just taken delivery of a new Beechcraft King Air 350 turboprop, eight passenger plane in October. Stephanie's mom called the company pilot and told him that she wanted to use the plane to fly to Lakeland, Florida on the 10th of November. She then called her husband, Frank, and informed him they were flying to Lakeland to find an appropriate venue for their daughter's wedding.

"No daughter of ours is going to get married in a justice of the peace office. It's bad enough that she is marrying below her station. I contacted a wedding planner in Lakeland for ideas for the wedding. She has made a reservation for us at The Terrace Hotel for four days."

As HAT recalled the story, on the morning of the 10th, he and Stephanie parked the '52 Ford pickup in the Anniston Municipal Airport parking lot and walked out to the new King Air 350 where the crew was loading her mother's luggage. It was a good thing they each had one small bag because the luggage compartment was almost full. They took off at 10 AM and one hour and thirty minutes later they were landing at Linder Airport in Lakeland.

The wedding planner met them, but her car was too small for the five of them and all their luggage. Harriet had packed like she was going to be away for weeks. She had outfits for daywear and nightwear with shoes and bags to match, plus jewelry and makeup.

HAT called Enterprise Rent-A-Car and rented a Ford van. He and Stephanie waited for the van to arrive while her parents left with the wedding planner. They arrived at The Terrace Hotel with the luggage in time to catch the ending of her mother's rant about the rooms being unacceptable.

"Don't you have a penthouse suite? That room on the third floor looking out over the street is totally unacceptable. Frank let's get out of this backwards country town and go to the Hilton in Tampa. I know they have suites."

Unperturbed, the desk attendant responded, "Ma'am, we have 15 suites. The ninth-floor suites have a beautiful view of Lake Mirror. I will be happy to have the bellman show them to you."

Mr. Stevens grew a backbone and assured the clerk that a suite on the ninth floor would be acceptable. If looks could kill, Mr. Stevens would be a dead man. Mrs. Stevens mumbled something under her breath as she walked towards the elevators. As they waited for the elevator to arrive Mr. Stevens asked his wife, "Harriet, why did you reserve three rooms? They lived together all summer."

Because of the cart full of luggage, HAT and Stephanie had to wait for another elevator. When HAT and Stephanie got to their eighth-floor rooms, Stephanie told HAT to take the key to his room back down to the desk clerk. When HAT returned to the room, Stephanie filled him in on a phone call with her mother.

"Mom said their suite is acceptable, but she would rather have gone to Tampa. She's complaining there can't be a decent place to eat in this 'backwater town'."

HAT reserved comment, knowing there was no good response and Stephanie continued, "Mom and Dad will meet us in the lobby in twenty minutes. The wedding planner will be back at 2:00 to go over her proposed plans." HAT began taking off his clothes and suggested Stephanie join him. They got down to the lobby twenty-five minutes later.

Stephanie ignored the stern look from Harriet and said, "There's an excellent restaurant just up the street which specializes in Cajun food. I know you like New Orleans cuisine, Mother."

"I can't imagine it will be worthwhile, but we must eat somewhere. It's too far to drive to Bern's Steakhouse in Tampa and get back by 2."

They walked up the street to Harry's Seafood Bar and Grille. It was a warm day, so they took a table outside looking over Munn Park. Harriet made small talk while they waited for their order. "There was a pamphlet in our suite that said our hotel was built in 1924. I guess you saw Lake Mirror from your window. Those flags along the promenade reflecting in the lake looked like a postcard."

HAT and Stephanie hadn't opened the curtains for obvious reasons, so Stephanie just nodded.

"The view reminded me of our trip to Europe last year. The pamphlet said the promenade was designed by Wilford Leavitt of New York and completed in 1928. It was named for a famous actress from Lakeland, Francis Langford. She was a big movie star back in the twenties. It seems that Lakeland was a popular winter vacation spot during the roaring '20s."

As Harriet talked, Frank sat quietly drinking his beer. When she took a breath and stopped talking for a second, Frank spoke up and asked HAT if he would take them on a tour of Lakeland.

"I'll be happy to. Did you know the corporate headquarters for a grocery store chain here in Florida called Publix is here in Lakeland?" HAT began, only to be interrupted by Harriet.

"It seems everyone, who is anyone, who comes to Lakeland, stays at The Terrace Hotel. Frank Lloyd Wright, Henry Ford and Frank Sinatra have stayed there. I guess we should reserve most of the rooms for the wedding or it may be full of peddlers selling to the grocery store or baseball players and fans in March."

"Do you think we will need 73 rooms and 15 suites, Mom?" Stephanie interjected.

"Darling, this is going to be the biggest wedding to happen in Lakeland in forever, so yes we will need most, if not all, of the rooms."

The food came and for the first time since they had sat down, Harriet was quiet. Halfway through her shrimp and grits, she spoke up again. "I can't believe I'm saying this, but this food is as good as I enjoyed in New Orleans. Stephanie, what do you think about having an outdoor wedding on the promenade next to Lake Mirror?"

After taking care of the check, Frank and HAT walked uptown to the Irish Pub for a beer while Harriet and Stephanie went back to the hotel for their meeting with the wedding planner.

"What are your plans after you finish with baseball? Frank asked.

"Well Mr. Stevens, I have a degree in physical education, so I guess I'll be a baseball coach somewhere. I'm investing my money and if I can play for ten years I should be able to live on a teacher's salary and be comfortable."

"If Stephanie is anything like her mother, you had better have a lot of money put back because she will be very high maintenance," Frank chuckled.

HAT thought, God help me if she turns out to be like her mother, thinking she is better than everyone else.

When Frank and HAT got back to the hotel, the wedding planner was finishing her presentation. "Frank, we need to reserve five suites and 50 rooms for three nights. There will be eight bridesmaids, two flower girls, four ushers, eight groomsmen, a best man and we will bring Reverend Hillsdale and his wife down to perform the ceremony."

Without pausing she continued, "You know anyone who's anyone in Anniston will want to attend. On second thought, Frank, reserve all the suites and rooms. We can always release them if we don't need them."

Of course, Sue and I were over the moon that HAT had finally made it official. As parents of the groom, and because we didn't travel in the same circles as the Stevens', we weren't asked what our thoughts or desires were for the upcoming nuptials. And we didn't mind. If HAT and Stephanie were happy, that was all that mattered to us.

CHAPTER 18

When we returned from our adventure to Russia, our lives returned to normal. No one in Anniston, not even Sue, would ever know we had smuggled the plans for the USSR's secret nuclear submarine out of Russia.

With tensions rising in the Middle East, we expected to be called up and deployed to support Operation Desert Shield, but a call never came. We continued to do our routine weekend training once a month at Maxwell hospital.

On the morning of January 17, 1991, JB and his squadron were part of a massive U.S. led air offensive that hit Iraq's air defenses, communication networks, weapon plants, and oil refineries. Operation Desert Shield was over, and Operation Desert Storm had begun. After 42 days of relentless attacks by the Allied Coalition air and ground forces, President George H.W. Bush declared a cease-fire on February 28th. Five days later, on March 5th, JB and his squadron departed Prince Sultan Air Base, Saudi Arabia and arrived back in Montgomery on the 7th to a hero's welcome.

In Lakeland, HAT and the Detroit Tigers were playing spring training games and getting ready for a wedding on March 15th which was an off day for the team.

The logistics of the Stevens–Talbert wedding rivaled the moving of the Ringling Bros. and Barnum & Bailey Greatest Show on Earth. About the only thing missing were the wild animals. Four days before the wedding, the decorating around Lake Mirror began: bleachers were moved in, a raft was anchored in the center of the lake where fireworks would be launched, a large tent was placed in the parking lot next to the Magnolia building where the reception would be held. Special lighting was set up all around the lake and the Magnolia building.

Mrs. Stevens wanted a search light to light up the night sky and one had to be brought in from Orlando. The sound system was installed and just about every florist in town had a contract to provide flowers. Rental cars were brought in from Orlando and Tampa. The largest catering company in Tampa was preparing the food for the reception. There was not a catering company in Lakeland that Mrs. Stevens trusted. A seamstress was on standby just in case some last-minute alterations were needed or an emergency with a dress occurred.

Mrs. Stevens hired a publicity director, who was busy making sure the local Lakeland newspaper, *The Ledger*, and the *Anniston Star*, the *Tampa Times*, *Orlando Sentinel* and *Detroit Free Press* had reporters and photographers covering the wedding. Most of the Detroit TV stations had sports reporters and camera crews in Lakeland covering spring training, but all the Detroit stations sent reporters just to handle the human-interest angle of one of their beloved Tigers.

Guests and members of the wedding party started to arrive on the 14th and were met by a film crew hired to memorialize the event. Invitees were coming by car, plane and two even came down from New York on the Amtrak train. Cars were running back and forth to Tampa International Airport and Orlando International Airport to ferry people to The Terrace Hotel. Wackenhut provided security. No one would get near the wedding without an invitation or a press pass. Mrs. Stevens was the ringmaster of this circus, and she loved it. She had long ago concluded that this was much better than a wedding at Saint Michael's All Angels Church. Meanwhile, Mr. Stevens was taking in the spring training games. His contribution to the wedding was signing the checks, of which there were many, and he would give away the bride. He was thankful he only had one daughter.

On the morning of the 14th Sue, and I, and eighteen friends who were going to the wedding waited at the Anniston Municipal airport for the 7:30 AM arrival of JB's C-47. A reporter and a photographer from the *Anniston Star* joined a reporter and a photojournalist from WJSU-TV, the Anniston TV station, alongside the Reverend and Mrs. Hillsdale in the parking lot. They would be flying down to Lakeland on the Stevens Company King Air which was also leaving at around the same time.

It was a chilly morning for this late in March, so most of those waiting for the planes stayed in their cars with the heaters running. They were all looking forward to getting to Lakeland where the afternoon high was predicted to be 85 degrees and sunny. Selma, JB and the twins arrived ten minutes early. After loading all the luggage and getting all the passengers strapped in, the plane was in the air by 8:00 with an estimated arrival time in Lakeland of 11:15.

From the air it was obvious where the city got its name: lakes dotted the landscape in every direction. Bringing the restored C-47 down to Lakeland for the annual SUN 'n FUN Aerospace Expo each April was on JB's bucket-list, but crop-dusting season always interfered.

JB and Selma landed smoothly at Lakeland Linder Airport and taxied to the general aviation area. The Stevens' King Air was already parked on the tarmac, having a cruising speed of 350 MPH, it took half as long to fly to Lakeland as the C-47. Sue and I exited the plane and were met by the reporter and photojournalist from WJSU-TV who were filming our arrival. It would be the lead for their report on the Stevens–Talbert wedding. A bus was on stand-by to take arrivals to The Terrace Hotel courtesy of Ring Master Harriet.

An Enterprise Rent-A-Car employee welcomed us with a sign for the "Farkenfield–Talbert Party" and directed us to a van that HAT had reserved. HAT was on his way to Winter Haven for a game against the Cleveland Indians and scheduled to pitch the first three innings. After checking into the hotel, we loaded back into the van for the drive to Winter Haven to watch HAT pitch. He allowed only two hits and no runs. When the next pitcher took the mound, HAT showered and changed and joined us in the stands to watch the rest of the game.

After the game, he and Tony headed to Orlando to pick up Mrs. Hatcher who flew in on Air Canada. Stephanie insisted that she be invited to the wedding and that HAT cover the cost of her ticket. Mrs. Hatcher met HAT and Tony with a big hug and a bag of her homemade peanut butter cookies. More than once on the trip to Lakeland she commented on how wonderful it was to be in balmy Florida and away from the cold of Canada. HAT made it to the rehearsal with time to spare.

The following evening the sky over Lake Mirror was shining from the search light as the invited guests waited for the arrival of the bride. HAT, eight groomsmen (the rest of the starting nine of the Detroit Tigers), eight bridesmaids, two flower girls, and me, HAT's best man, joined Reverend Hillsdale waiting anxiously for the arrival of the bride.

Her father escorted Stephanie down a set of steps to the promenade as the melody of the Wedding March filled the air. HAT's heart skipped a few beats as he watched his bridge approach and stand next to him. His mind was a blur as Reverend Hillsdale conducted the ceremony. When the good reverend said, "I pronounce you man and wife. What God has joined together let no man put asunder. You may kiss your bride," fireworks lit up the sky.

After kissing his bride, HAT and Stephanie led their guests across the street to the Magnolia building where the wedding reception was being held. The ten-piece, tuxedo-clad, orchestra played while the guests enjoyed hors d'oeuvres and found their seats. Soon the main course arrived, and the room was filled with happy chatter. After the usual reception protocols and much drinking and dancing it came time for the bride and groom to leave. The eight groomsmen formed an arch of baseball bats for the newlyweds as they walked to the waiting limousine which whisked them away to their short two-night honeymoon.

CHAPTER 19

We slept late the morning after the wedding and joined JB, Selma, and the twins for lunch and a tour of Lakeland. A block from the hotel, at the corner of Main and Kentucky, was Munn Park. Well-maintained buildings dating back to the '20s surrounded the park, and like The Terrace and the promenade, conveyed a special charm of past glory. Large oak trees provided shade from the bright Florida sun and added to the small-town ambiance. Too many of these downtown areas in small towns had dried up and fell into disrepair as malls were built, but downtown Lakeland had morphed into a destination area of bars, restaurants, ice cream parlors, specialty shops, and office buildings.

It was a warm afternoon and we decided to have lunch at Harry's Bar. We requested seating at a patio table overlooking the park where we could people-watch. JB and I ordered his favorite, shrimp and grits. Selma chose the shrimp and scallop Evangeline and Sue, who was always watching her weight, ordered a large salad. The twins found nothing appealing and headed down the street for pizza.

We enjoyed a leisurely meal soaking in the atmosphere and catching up with our old friends. After looking over the dessert menu, Selma ordered Bananas Foster. "JB, do you remember where we were when we first had Bananas Foster?" she asked.

"That would be at the Victoria Falls Hotel in Rhodesia the weekend I asked you to marry me," JB answered, proud that he remembered. "How about you, Right, would you like some dessert? I think I'm going to order some key lime pie and a cup of coffee."

"Sounds good, I'll take the same."

While waiting for their dessert to arrive, JB reached into his jacket pocket, "I picked up this tourist map in the lobby and there are some interesting places to see in and around Lakeland. Why don't we pile into the van and see the sites this afternoon?"

We settled the check and rose to leave when a man at the next table stood, "Excuse me, but did I see you all come into the airport yesterday morning on a DC-3?" he asked.

"Guilty as charged, that's our tail dragger," JB responded.

"That's one beautiful airplane. Someone did an excellent job of restoration."

"Thank you. It was a labor of love and money, and the best mechanic this side of the pond. I'm JB Farkenfield, this is my wife, Selma, and friends of ours, Robert and Sue Talbert. We have two daughters around here somewhere."

"It's a pleasure to meet y'all. My name is Phil Carter. I'm a pilot for Publix and would love to see the inside of it sometime. Are you here for the wedding?"

"Yes, we're the groom's parents," Sue replied.

"Well, congratulations. The whole town was excited about that wedding. It was quite a production. There was a front-page story in *The Ledger* this morning and it was on the sports news on the early show on channel 11. It's not every day that the star pitcher of the Detroit Tigers gets married in Lakeland. I saw him pitch his first professional game here in Lakeland. You must be immensely proud of him."

"Thank you, Phil, we are. So, you're a baseball fan?" I replied.

"Yes sir, the Tigers are the pride and joy of Lakeland."

We started to excuse ourselves when JB stopped and turned back to Phil's table. "Phil, if you're interested, we're flying down to Key West in the morning. If you're at the airport around 0900 I'll give you a tour of the plane and if you'd like, you can come along for the ride."

"That's mighty generous of you JB and I'd really enjoy that tour. The invitation to the Keys is tempting. Would you mind if I bring my sister, Pam?"

"The more the merrier, Phil. See you at nine."

After locating the twins and a quick trip to our rooms, we met at the entrance to the hotel where the valet had the van waiting. "I'll drive," I said to JB, "You have the map, where to first?"

"Let's start with Florida Southern College and give Jane and Julie a tour of the campus. It's never too early for them to start looking at colleges. According to the tour guide, the FSC campus boasts the largest number of Frank Lloyd Wright structures in the United States."

As we were driving to the campus, we passed Lake Morton which was home to the famous Lakeland swans. Selma insisted that we stop so she could get pictures. Sue read the tour guide:

> *"Lakeland has been known for its swans as far back as 1923. In 1953 the last two swans disappeared, probably dinner for a hungry alligator. The people of Lakeland were devastated, and a reporter wrote a story about the disappearance of the swans.*

> *Mr. and Mrs. Pickhurt, Lakeland natives stationed at an Air Force Base in England, received a copy of the article from her mother and Mrs. Pickhurt had the audacity to write to Queen Elizabeth requesting a pair of royal swans be donated to the city of Lakeland.*

> *To Mrs. Pickhurt's great surprise, the Queen agreed if Lakeland paid for all the expenses of transporting the swans from London to Lakeland. After a fund drive, the required $300 was raised and the two royal mute swans were released on Lake Morton on February 9, 1957.*

> *This time the city ensured no alligators got near Lake Morton and the population of swans quickly grew to over eighty swans. Every October the swans are checked by a veterinarian and the excess swans are sold."*

"What a charming story," Selma commented.

At the FSC campus, we admired the Frank Lloyd Wright buildings overlooking Lake Hollingsworth where students were water skiing. Back in Alabama it was 43 degrees and raining but here it was 81 degrees and a bright sunny day. The twins were sold. This was the college for them. They would change their minds many times before they graduated from high school.

After the tour of Florida Southern, knowing it was one of the twins' favorite pastimes on sizzling summer Alabama days, JB suggested they drive over to Winter Haven and visit Cypress Gardens to watch the water ski show.

From the back row of the van, Jane asked, "Was water skiing invented at Cypress Gardens? You see Cypress Gardens water skis, ski belts, bathing suits, even Cypress Garden ski boats."

Sue paged through the tour guide until she found the answer:

"Water skiing was invented by a man named Ralph Samuelson in 1922 in Lake City, Minnesota. Dick Pope, who owned Cypress Gardens until his death, started the water ski show as an added attraction to the gardens. He persuaded Arthur Godfrey, who had a TV show in the fifties, to broadcast from the Gardens and attendance skyrocketed. Up until Disney World, it had the highest attendance of any tourist attraction in Florida."

JB caught Jane's eye in the rear-view mirror, "When I was fourteen years old my family took a long road trip through Florida, and we stopped at Cypress Gardens. I remember being enthralled by the skiers. It looked like so much fun I was determined to learn, but unfortunately the nearest body of water to Anniston was 80 miles away and my father refused to buy a ski boat. By the time I was a junior in high school Alabama Power built that dam on the Coosa River near Anniston and created the large reservoir, perfect for water skiing. Next to flying, water skiing was my favorite activity. Right Hand, you remember that small wooden ski boat?"

Laughing, I responded, "How could I forget," turning to the twins I continued the story, "My neighbor built it from a plan in a *Popular Mechanics* magazine and gave it to us because his wife wanted it out of his garage so she could park her car inside. Your Dad, George Daniel and I spent every Saturday from September to the next May working on that boat. We found an old 40 horsepower outboard motor for $50, and the seller threw in a boat trailer which had two flat tires we had to replace before we could take it home. The first warm Saturday in May we hooked up the trailer to George's car and headed for the lake. By sundown that day we were able to get up on skis and almost make a complete round of the lake before we fell. Every weekend from May until late October we were at the lake skiing."

"I guess Jane and Julia got their love of water skiing indirectly from the Cypress Gardens water ski show," Selma suggested.

"Did you ever get your share of the money when George sold the boat the summer Sue and I got orders for Japan?" I asked JB.

"Nope, not a cent," JB replied. A brief shadow crossed his face as he recalled that while he was a POW the debt was impossible to repay.

The twins loved the ski show and vowed they were going to join the cast someday.

Saturday morning, we arrived at the airport to find eight bridesmaids waiting for the trip to Key West. The C-47 had 24 passenger seats and two jump seats, so all passenger seats weren't full when Phil and Pam arrived just before nine. Selma and JB had done their preflight walk around and were ready to load up and take off for Key West.

Phil couldn't get over how well the plane had been maintained. "We have the best aircraft mechanic this side of the Mississippi working for us," JB explained, "Selma and I are agricultural pilots. We own a crop-dusting service in North Alabama."

As they boarded, JB offered Phil one of the jump seats up front. When the plane was built back in 1944, it was the navigator's seat, but JB had updated the navigation system with the latest technology and had no need for a navigator.

Phil explained that he had been an Air Force pilot and started flying for Publix when he retired. "Corporate flying doesn't pay as well as the airlines, but I'm home every night."

Selma, our pilot for the day, suggested Phil take the co-pilot seat instead. "Once we're in flight you can fly part of the way to Key West and get the feel of flying a true pioneer passenger aircraft." Thrilled at the offer, Phil settled in beside her and started to examine the controls and instrument panel while JB made himself comfortable in the jump seat.

Selma started the right engine, which as usual backfired and spewed a cloud of black smoke. After a few seconds, it was running smoothly. Then she fired up the left engine which did the same. I laughed as I watched the bridesmaids who were clearly wondering if they'd made a good decision about the trip to Key West.

Selma keyed her mic, "This is your Captain speaking. You should be in your seats with your seat belts buckled. We will be taking off for Key West shortly. Our flying time today is one hour and twenty minutes. I will turn off the seat belt sign when we get to our cruising altitude of 6,000 feet. Our flight attendants will then come through the cabin with snacks. Jane and Julie, you have the duty on today's flight."

She radioed the tower and asked permission to roll out onto the taxiway. "Tango Foxtrot C-47 263 you are cleared to proceed to runway 10/28. You are second in line behind the Piper Cub."

"Roger that, Tango Foxtrot C 47 263 is rolling onto the taxiway and proceeding to runway 10/28."

Switching back to her onboard channel, Selma informed her passengers, "We are second in line for takeoff from runway 10/28 and should be in the air in only a few minutes. Please sit back and enjoy your flight. Thank you for flying Chocwataw Airlines today."

Once the Piper was airborne the tower radioed, "Tango Foxtrot C-47 263 you are cleared for takeoff. Have a good trip."

With that, Selma poured the coal to the engines and the plane started to vibrate. She released the brakes, and the old DC-3 began its roll down the runway. It soon broke its hold on the ground and started a slow climb into the sky. Selma banked right and pointed the plane towards Key West. When they reached 6,000 feet, she turned off the seat belt sign and told Jane and Julie to serve their guests coffee. She looked over at Phil and asked him if he would like to fly the old lady.

"Yes, but it has been a long time since I flew a reciprocating engine plane and never this size."

"She's quite easy to fly, you'll quickly get the hang of it. JB come take my seat, I need to hit the head. I had too much coffee at breakfast."

The March morning sky was clear, not a cloud in the sky, and it was a smooth flight to Key West. When Key West International Airport came into view, JB contacted air traffic control for permission to land.

"Tango Foxtrot C-47 263 you are cleared to land on runway 09/27. Our runway is only 5,076 feet long, but you shouldn't have any problem landing your DC-3."

"Roger that."

JB announced, "Everyone should be in your seats with your seat belt buckled in preparation for landing in Key West. We should be on the ground in a few minutes."

After a perfect landing JB taxied to the general aviation area where he was told to park next to a Cessna Crusader. As we exited the plane, I noticed the Cessna which looked familiar. Selma requested everyone be back at the airport no later than 10 PM for takeoff promptly at 10:30 for arrival in Lakeland at midnight.

"If you're late, you'll have to make your own arrangements to get home. Do you all understand?" she asked, speaking directly to the bridesmaids and the twins.

"Be back by 10:30, we understand," the bridesmaids replied in unison.

"That's not what I said," she said to the girls.

"We'll be back at 10," the maid-of-honor assured her.

With that, the bridal party was off to explore Key West. Phil wanted to check out the Cessna and as we walked up to the plane, the passenger door opened. The man at the top of the stairs was no stranger.

Art Nathanson/Gill Maxwell walked down the steps and came straight to our group. He gave Selma a kiss on the cheek and bear-hugged JB. He then turned to Sue and me and did the same. We were all confused, but for different reasons.

"Of all the gin mills in all the cities, what is the chance that I would run into y'all in Key West, Florida," he exclaimed, grasping JB's shoulder. "What's it been? Twenty years since I last saw you and Selma. When I looked out the window and saw the C-47 come to a stop, I thought I recognized it. I can't believe that it's still flying but Slim is the best aircraft mechanic that I ever came across."

JB cast a quick glance at Selma, who nodded. "You're right on the money, Slim's a miracle worker with a plane engine." Right Hand didn't miss the glance to Selma and JB now caught his eye. The unspoken message was clear, he had no idea I had encountered Gill in my past.

My immediate concern was Sue. I had never divulged the true reason for our work with *International Traveler* magazine. Certainly, Gill knew that, and I had no idea how this encounter would play out, but I had no doubt it wasn't a coincidence.

JB bought me some time, "Selma and I last saw you twenty-two years ago. We settled down in North Alabama. These are our girls, Jane and Julie, and it appears you already know Robert and Sue."

"A pleasure to meet you girls. And let me make amends for your father's lack of manners, my name's Art Nathanson."

I'm positively certain Sue heard my heavy sigh of relief, but she still appeared to be lost in how all these relationships revolved around Art/Gill.

"Did you know our mother when she was a fighter pilot in Rhodesia?" Jane asked.

"I sure did. I introduced your dad to your mother."

Forgive me the bad manners, Art, let me introduce you to Phil and Pam Carter. Art is an old friend. I worked for him as an agriculture pilot when he had a contract in Rhodesia."

"Nice to meet you," he said as he shook Phil's hand.

Sue seemed to be putting pieces together, "Art, you never mentioned you were in the crop-dusting business."

"Sure was. A long time ago. Never seemed to come up in any of our conversations. After my contract in Rhodesia, I came back to the States and decided to do something different. I loved travel and when I saw an opportunity to do it on someone else's dime I went to work for *International Traveler*."

I was in awe of how seamlessly Art/Gill wove a cover, but of course he'd probably been doing it his entire adult life. It was also clear that JB and Selma were no strangers to going with the flow when it came to identities and backstories.

"I'm on a stop coming back from Cartagena, Colombia working on a proposed story for our July issue. I need to be back in the air in about an hour, but I would love to have a drink and catch up. I know it's early, but as they say, 'It must be five o'clock somewhere', and when in Key West it's always party time."

We all seemed happy with that plan. I knew I could use a cold beer right about that time. "How does Sloppy Joe's Bar, Hemingway's favorite drinking spot in Key West, sound?" he suggested.

"Lead the way," JB said.

"Hold on just a minute, I need to grab something from the plane," Art/Gill climbed the stairs and disappeared into the Cessna, quickly rejoining the group holding a copy of the latest issue of *International Traveler* and handed it to JB. "Turn to page 36 and read the title of the article."

"Traveling with the Talberts: Mystery Meat, Cabbage and Potatoes, Our Tour of Russia" JB read the headline.

"Damn, why didn't you tell us you're celebrities?" JB asked, turning to Right and Sue.

"We weren't sure our article would get published so we didn't make a big deal about it," Right explained.

Selma was the next one to smooth out some wrinkles. "JB, you remember Right told us about their trip to Russia and writing that article for a magazine, don't you? What are the odds that the person they worked for is the man responsible for our being together. It's such a small world."

Small world wasn't how I'd describe it, but okay. I was new to this subterfuge game, but I knew in my gut there was more to this encounter than met the eye. The mention of Cartegena wasn't lost on me. As we walked down Duval Street, the ladies stopped at an antique shop, telling us they would catch up. If it weren't for the presence of Phil, I could have questioned our mutual covert friend about the true nature of this impromptu visit, but that would have to wait for a more appropriate time. A few shops later, Gill stopped to read a poster in the window.

"Hey JB, look at this, you're not going to believe it."

Country Fest
Saturday, March 17
Ricky Van Shelton and Jean Auburndale
Sunday, March 18
Diamond Rio and Brooks and Dunn
The Truman Waterfront Park Amphitheater
Entertainment starts at 7:30 p.m.

"Isn't that a kicker. First, you show up out of my past and now Jean's in town," JB observed.

"Who's Jean Auburndale?" I asked.

When JB didn't answer, Art/Gill filled in the blanks. "JB and Jean had a history together before he met Selma. He picked her up when Jean was hitchhiking and she stayed with him at his cabin on Lake Chocwataw for a while before she went on to Nashville and hit it big."

"It wasn't serious." JB protested.

"Don't listen to him, folks thought they would get married," Art/Gill countered. I realized that Gill knew intimate details about JB's life long before their time in Rhodesia, details I didn't know.

"Okay, I might have fallen for her, but I knew our lives would take off in different directions and I was a few years older, which seemed to be problem for her. Anyway, she ended up married to a guy in her band while I was in Rhodesia."

We walked into Sloppy Joe's Bar and the gods of relationships past were raining on JB that day because sitting at a corner table was none other than JB's old flame, Jean Auburndale. She saw JB before he saw her and in seconds was on him like white on rice, grabbing him in a passionate embrace and slapping a wet kiss on his lips. JB got untangled from her and stepped back.

Standing off to the side, I thought it was a good thing Selma wasn't here to witness that, and then I noticed that Ms. Auburndale wasn't wearing a wedding ring.

"I can't believe you just walked in here," she exclaimed. "You look great!" She suddenly realized JB was with a few friends and included us in the conversation. "We haven't seen each other since my show in Birmingham after JB came back from Rhodesia."

Focusing back on JB, she continued, "A lot of water's flowed under the bridge since then, huh. Hey, are you and Selma still together? I just divorced my third husband."

Back to the group who stood silent, "I keep saying yes to the wrong men. I should have said yes to the right man twenty-two years ago when he asked me," she said with a wink and a nod in JB's direction.

"Come on over and sit," she said as she headed back to her table, "Grab a few more chairs and join me for lunch."

"To answer your question, yes, Selma and I are still together. She'll be here in a few minutes, with our daughters."

That piece of news seemed to take a bit of wind out of Ms. Auburndale's sails.

"This is my friend, Right Hand, and a fellow pilot, Phil Carter, and the one and only Gill Maxwell. You may remember me working for him back in the day."

"You're the one who kept taking JB away from me to go fly in those God forsaken places. That led to my first mistake in the marriage department. Let's get a bigger table where we can all sit down and catch up on the last twenty years."

Through the window I saw the girls approaching and I knew the jig was up when Phil said, "I thought your name was Art."

Selma took in the scene, including lipstick all over JB's mouth, and didn't look so happy. Pam went all gushy and asked for Jean's autograph which Jean was happy to give. This got the twins all excited and amidst the commotion I noticed JB and Gill take Phil aside and Gill slip out the front door.

"You all must order the Sloppy Joe special. You know that Sloppy Joes were invented here," Jean effused.

JB approached and slapped me on the shoulder, "All good with you, Right?"

"Uh-huh."

"Yes, Right, it's all good."

"Okay, if you say so."

With that we put a couple of tables together and joined our country star for lunch. Conversation was flowing with Jean regaling the twins with stories of stars she's met and worked with. Shortly after ordering, Sue, sitting between me and JB, asked. "Where's Art?"

"He lost track of time and had to get back to the plane, but we'll make plans to get together for a proper reunion soon," JB said smoothly. I was starting to wonder how many layers there were to my friend and how well I knew the man he had become.

Once it was clear Selma's claim on JB was iron-clad, Jean stopped flirting and JB brought her up to date on their lives.

Jean was clearly never short for words and after listening to her lengthy monologue you could sum up her life with; she was still writing songs, recording and touring, and divorcing husbands.

"I bought George and Tammy's house out on 540A in Lakeland, and moved my parents in. I stay there in the winter when I'm not recording in Nashville or on tour. I came down to Key West yesterday to rehearse with a local band who'll be backing me tonight at Country Fest. It's a lot cheaper to use a local band than fly my regular band down from Nashville. I still get paid my normal fee for a two-hour show but more goes into my bank account. I can get you all stage passes if you would like to see the show."

I marveled that Jean hadn't taken a breath, but I suppose being a singer, a surplus of lung capacity comes with the territory. Seated across the table, Jane looked enthralled, and I heard Julie inform Selma that she wasn't going to join the cast of Cypress Gardens. Instead, she wanted a guitar, and she was going to write songs and be a country-music star.

JB responded to Jean's offer, "There are 16 of us. We have eight bridesmaids wandering around Key West somewhere. We don't want to impose."

"Oooh, bridesmaids! Who's getting married?" Jean asked excited at the prospect of another wedding.

"My son got married yesterday in Lakeland," Sue answered. From the tone of her voice, I could tell she wasn't taken in by the aura of fame and fortune.

"Well, I'm sure I can get tickets for everyone. I go on at nine and the show ends at eleven if y'all are going to be in town tonight."

Selma, who had said little throughout lunch, spoke up, "I'm sorry, but thanks for the offer. We take off at 10:30."

"No problem, I'll call the band and tell them to show up for the 7:30 show and I'll perform at 7:30 instead of 9:00. Ricky won't mind the switch. He'll be able to tell his friends back in Nashville that Jean Auburndale opened for him. Will that give you time to make your scheduled take-off? Is it a date?"

Clearly, Jean wouldn't take no for an answer and Pam and Phil expressed their desire to see the show, so we all agreed. We would meet at 5 PM at Mallory Square to watch the sunset and head over to the concert from there.

After walking and biking around Key West the rest of the afternoon it was a relief to sit on a bench and watch the breathtaking sunset. We were at the southern-most point of the United States, with the communist island of Cuba only 90 miles south across the Straits of Florida.

The crowd in the square was an eclectic group. Street performers entertained people of all shapes, sizes, and shades, who were enjoying what mother nature provided for a finale to a beautiful day.

We had just enough time to grab something to eat before heading for Country Fest. Jean sang some of her old songs, "I-75 Blues", "When the Sun Goes Down in Florida", "Doublewides and Cheap Wine", and "Welfare Payday". All songs that she had written back when she and JB were together. She closed the show with a song she dedicated to an old friend, "Midnight in Gainesville".

with a song she dedicated to an old friend, "Midnight in Gainesville".

CHAPTER 20

Before leaving spring training for Detroit, HAT and Stephanie bought a lot on Eagle Lake in a new gated HOA community called Eagles Landing. The contractor estimated he could have the house finished by December. As HAT had a great season, Shephanie and her mother used the company plane to fly back and forth to Lakeland to oversee the construction.

At the end of the season, HAT was a free agent and could sign with the highest bidder. He re-signed with the Tigers and became a rich young man. Endorsement deals with a cereal company and Aqua Velva were secured and his face was on cereal boxes all over the world and in TV ads on all the channels.

While HAT was enjoying his success, I was tired of rolling pills. I lost interest in the store and spent most of my time at the cabin on the river. I soon tired of fishing and felt I needed something to fill my life with meaning. With the fall of the USSR, there were fewer Bible smuggling trips, and we hadn't been called to write another travel article. One night while eating dinner Sue suggested that I go back to school to get my teachers certificate.

"You used to talk about how you wanted to teach science. Why don't you do it? I'm sure you would enjoy it more than running the pharmacy. Your assistant can run the pharmacy while you go to school, and you can work on Saturdays. If you enjoy teaching, sell the pharmacy. Maybe your assistant will want to buy it. I read an article in the *Air Force Times* about a program for retirees called 'Troops to Teachers'. The government pays your tuition, books and fees, and pays a small stipend for two years while you are in school getting your teacher's certificate. When you go to work, they pay seventy-five percent of your first year's salary, fifty-percent the second year, and twenty-five percent the third year."

As usual, what Sue was saying made a lot of sense. "You know, I think that's a good plan. The goal will be to simplify my life. I've been thinking of putting in my retirement papers with the Reserves. As a full Colonel I'm required to fly up to D.C. every month for my weekend duty and I miss being with you."

"I don't enjoy being away from you either," Sue said, taking my hand, "We've both served our country well and it may be time to pass the torch to the younger generation. Why don't we both put in our papers? We have enough good years to retire comfortably."

So that was the plan, but before I retired, I applied and was accepted into the Troops to Teachers program.

I had a choice of where to study. Bradford University was only 35 miles from our cabin in Saint Clair County, but it was a private university, and its tuition was more than the 3T program would pay. Northeast Alabama State College was just 16 miles southeast of the cabin. Northeast State was a holdover from the time of segregation when there were separate colleges for whites and blacks. Once desegregation came about, these state schools continued to operate as historically all black institutions (HCBUs) of higher learning. My tax money was paying for this school, so I decided to apply.

I was accepted and started school during the fall quarter. When I drove through the gate entering Northeast Alabama State College, I noticed there were no whites walking around the campus. The lady in the registration office asked me why I was there, and I showed her my acceptance letter. She looked at the letter and back at me, then she said, "You're not black, are you?"

"No ma'am, I'm not." I knew some people who considered themselves black who were as white as I am so I could understand her question. Her next question surprised me, "If you're not black, why are you coming to Northeast Alabama State?"

"Well, one reason is it's an accredited state college only 16 miles from my back door. The other is, I've worked with and for blacks for the past 30 years, so I don't see any reason not to attend Northeast Alabama State."

"Then I suppose I should welcome you to Northeast, Mr. Talbert. But I should tell you that you will be the only white student this year: a minority of one."

After getting my ID card, I bought my books and sat down on a bench outside the student union to watch the students. They reminded me of my time as an undergrad at Auburn. Boys were scoping out the girls and the girls were checking out the boys. There were the cool dudes, girls who knew they were hot, and a few nerds. It was just like the first day on campus of any college. The only difference was, apart from me, all the students were black. A young man sat down next to me and asked if I was a professor.

"No, I'm not a professor."

"Then what are you?" he asked.

"Are you always this inquisitive, asking personal questions of people you don't know?" I replied.

"I'm sorry, I don't mean to be rude, but you seem to be out of place."

Laughing, I said, "Is it because of my age that you think I am out of place?"

He smiled and stated the obvious, "No, it's because you are white."

"Robert Talbert," I said offering my hand, which he shook. "I'm a student, just enrolled. I presume you are also?"

Without offering an introduction, he said, "You can't be a student; you're not black, and this is a black college."

"Well, I hate to disappoint you, but I am a student, and this is a state-supported school which is required to admit anyone qualified for admission, regardless of race." When he didn't reply, I asked, "If you can go to the University of Alabama, why can't I attend Northeast State? I was around your age when the Civil Rights Act of 1964 was passed, which I'm sure your grandparents fought for. That gave you and I the right to attend any college of our choice. What's your name, son?"

"Nate Sherman. Family name supposedly comes from being a decedent of General Sherman."

"Well, he served this young country well during and after the Civil War, so if that's the case you should be proud. You do know he was white."

"Man, you do know there's a whole lot of black people with white blood, don't you?"

"That's a fact. It's a pleasure to meet you Nate Sherman, and I hope we talk again soon." I excused myself and wandered around the campus a bit longer before heading home.

Having a BS degree, I didn't have to take any of the required courses and my major was in Middle School Education which would allow me to teach any course in grades five thru nine. With the courses I took for my BS, and the courses they gave me credit for from Air War College, I had enough credits for a major in Social Studies, Math, and English. I needed a physical science course to be able to teach science, so I registered for a physics course, an English writing course, and a "How to Teach Math" course. This would be the first of many "How to Teach" courses. When I walked into the 8 AM physics course most of the seats were empty so I had my choice. I took a seat in the front row, took out a notebook and pencil and prepared to take notes. A few more students drifted in, but 8 AM came and went and no professor showed up. I didn't know the rule at Northeast State but at Auburn you waited on an instructor for ten minutes and a full professor for twenty. A few more students dragged in and flopped down in their seats. At 8:19, Doctor Jefferson, Ph.D., a full professor, walked into the class.

He handed out a paper outlining the course, his grading scale and the dates of the midterm and final exams. He explained we would have a lab every Friday where we would work with a lab partner to solve a physics problem. He took a big swig from his coffee mug then told us to choose a lab partner and he would see us tomorrow and he walked out.

Most of the students turned away when I walked up to them to ask if they wanted to be lab partners. I got the feeling that the old white guy was being shunned. How dare he invade a black-only domain. I started to leave when a young man approached me, introduced himself and asked if I would be his lab partner. I introduced myself and thanked him for asking me and said that I thought we would make a good team.

Since I had forty minutes before my English class, I decided to go to the Student Union to get something to drink. I asked my lab partner to join me, but he declined because he was meeting his girlfriend. I got a coffee and sat down to observe the students as they came and went.

"Excuse me, you're in my 8 AM physics class, mind if I sit down?" It was Doctor Jefferson, Ph.D., full professor.

"Feel free," I said offering him a chair.

"I was just wondering what a middle-aged white man was doing in a physics class at Northeast State?" he asked.

"Getting certified to teach middle school students," I answered.

"I'm like Paul Harvey, I want to know the rest of the story, if you don't mind," he said.

I took a sip of my coffee before answering. "I worked as a pharmacist for many years and got tired of the grind, so I decided to find something where I could contribute to the good of mankind. President Clinton established a program called Troops to Teachers and just before I retired from the Air Force Reserves I applied and got accepted. Northeast State is 16 miles from my back door, so here I am. You know, you're the third person to ask me what I am doing at Northeast State. I'm starting to get the feeling that I'm not welcome."

"Well, Mr. Talbert, you're like a turd in a punch bowl. You'll get a lot of attention, but not too many people will associate with you. Did you get anyone to be your lab partner?"

"Yes, a nice young man by the name of Fred Davis."

"Good. Fred is the son of Dr. Davis in the music department. He is a very smart young man. You probably have the best lab partner you could get." He rose and excused himself, "I need to get my handouts distributed to my 9:00 class. I'll see you tomorrow."

My next class was English writing. The professor was on time but there were several students who wandered in late. I was starting to see a trend. There didn't seem to be any repercussions for being late, so the students came in whenever they wanted, if they came in at all. I assumed the professors felt that since the students paid their money they could care less if they came to class.

Later I learned that many of the students had Federal Pell grants which paid for their tuition, books, and room and board. Some students never came to class. During an audit the following quarter, federal auditors discovered fraud and the school was fined for laxity in managing the Pell program. By summer quarter there was a new President of the school and roll was taken in each class with repercussions for being late to class and unexcused absences.

The English writing professor gave us a writing assignment to be turned in at the next class. I filled up two pages with bullshit of why I wanted to be a teacher and who had most influenced me to go into education. We got our papers back at the beginning of our Thursday class. My paper had an A+ at the top of the page and a note to see the professor after class. The first words out of her mouth were, "Mr. Talbert, why are you in my writing class? You are wasting your time. You don't have to come to class anymore if you don't want to. I'll give you an A+ as a final grade."

"Are you sure?" I asked, confused.

"Your writing is beyond where most students will be at the end of my course. Would you tell me why you are attending Northeast State?

The thought crossed my mind that I should type up a card explaining why I was attending Northeast State which I could hand to people when I met them. For the fourth time in a week, I explained my reason for attending Northeast State.

At the Friday physics lab, Fred and I finished our problem early. On Monday we got our papers back and our grade was 100. As we were leaving class a student asked Fred what grade he made. Several students overheard Fred's answer and I heard someone say, "I should have asked you to be my lab partner."

In next Friday's lab we were working on our problem and two guys kept coming over and watching what we were doing and then going back to their partners. Monday, we found out we aced another lab and the two guys who had been copying off us also had 100s. As we left class it was clear Fred was upset that the cheaters got a grade they didn't earn.

Over coffee in the Student Union, I suggested a plan that would stop the copying of our papers. "Friday, we'll work the problem wrong and let them copy it, then we'll correct our work and turn it in."

The next lab we put my plan into action and the two guys copied the wrong computations. We then changed our answers and turned in our paper. Monday, we got our papers back and we had another 100. As we walked out of class the two cheaters stopped Fred and chided him about not acing the lab this time. Fred asked why they thought he didn't get a 100. "Well, we failed," one of the two geniuses admitted. Fred laughed, "Mr. Talbert found our mistake before we turned in the paper and changed it." The next Friday they copied someone else's work.

We had our midterm exam and when Professor Jefferson returned the papers there were many "Oh shits" and moans and groans heard around the room. I earned an A+, 100. One of the students asked Professor Jefferson if he had changed his policy of taking the highest grade made on the test, subtracting it from 100, and adding that amount to everyone's paper.

"No change, that's still my policy," Jefferson confirmed.

"Then there's some kind of mistake because you didn't add anything to my grade," the inquiring mind stated.

"That's right I didn't."

"But you just said you hadn't changed your policy."

"That's right, I haven't changed my policy."

"But you didn't add anything to my grade."

"No, I didn't."

Fred spoke up and said, "Dumb ass, someone made a 100."

Twenty-three faces turned and stared at me knowing Fred had made a 98. After my last class, I approached my truck and found someone had keyed it all the way down the right side. Welcome to Northeast State old white man. At the end of the quarter, I had three As and a truck with a scratch down the right side. At least no one had tarred and feathered me.

Winter quarter I signed up for Teaching Reading, Teaching Social Studies, Classroom Management, and Middle School Psychology. Two weeks into the quarter my Teaching Reading professor, Professor Higgins, stopped me in the Student Union. He wanted to talk to me about why I was attending Northeast State. I really should have typed up the card to give to people who asked me that question. I gave him the Paul Harvey answer so now he knew the rest of the story.

About the same time that I enrolled at Northeast State I began volunteering in a fifth-grade remedial reading class at our local elementary school. Higgins said that he lived next door to the principal of the school, and the principal told him I was doing an excellent job with the students who were below grade level in reading. I explained to Professor Higgins that I was using a program I had read about called "Accelerated Reading".

"The article claimed schools that are using it are having phenomenal results in improving reading. The Gadsden city school system had installed Accelerated Reading in all their schools. I was curious, so I contacted a school which had been using the program for the past year and they invited me to come down and observe. It might be good to take our class to see what they are doing."

He agreed so I set up the visit and Professor Higgins got the Northeast Alabama State Wild Cats bus to transport the class to Gadsden.

Not long after that visit, Professor Higgins wanted to see me. He felt that I was learning more in the classroom working with the fifth graders than he could teach me, and I didn't need to come back to his class. He suggested I keep a diary of what I was doing as a volunteer and turn it in to him once a week and confirmed that my grade for the course was an A+.

My professor for Classroom Management was another Ph.D. Dr. Phillips was one of the best instructors that I ever had. He took what could have been a very dry subject and using case studies kept everyone involved. He told us the first day we walked into a classroom we must have a classroom management plan. He said classroom management is more important than lesson plans. If you can't manage your classroom, you can't teach and if you can't teach, your students can't learn.

Dr. Phillips had earned his degree in Education from Northeast State and after graduating he took a job in a small rural elementary school in Dooling, Georgia. His first day in the classroom, a boy walked out of the class and using the downspout pipe on the side of the building, climbed up on the roof and sat down. The children in class were going crazy watching from the windows. Dr. Phillips couldn't get them to quiet down. As he tells it, Phillips lined up the students and marched them outside where he could see them all.

Then, he tried to talk the boy down off the roof, but the kid refused to come down. Dooling is in the red clay part of Georgia, and this gave Dr. Phillips an idea of how to get the boy off the roof. He told the boy if he didn't come down, he was going to hit him with a dirt clod. The boy laughed and Dr. Phillips picked up a dirt clod and threw it at him, but the boy dodged and laughed some more and said, "You can't hit me."

Dr. Phillips told the other 29 students to pick up a dirt clod and they would all throw them at the same time. On the count of three, 30 dirt clods filled the air, and the boy couldn't dodge them all. The boy must have been hit by at least half the clods. If you have ever been hit by a Georgia red clay dirt clod, you know that the boy was not having the best of times. Dr. Phillips said he asked the boy if he was ready to climb down now or the class was going to reload and let fly another volley of dirt clods. The boy decided it was in his best interest to climb down.

The point of Dr. Phillips' story was we had to be prepared for whatever happened in the classroom. He said he didn't recommend throwing dirt clods at a student, but we would have to face all kinds of situations in the classroom and must be able to think quickly to control the situation.

Dr. Phillips had grown up in the black part of his hometown. Like my hometown, the blacks and the poor whites lived near the polluting industries that took advantage of Southern towns. The plant near his home spewed poison into the air that caused cancer. A class action suit was brought against the company, but Dr. Phillips died halfway through spring quarter. I wasn't the only white person at his funeral.

During spring quarter, I did my practice teaching and took the state exam to get my teacher's certificate. County school systems came to Northeast State near the end of the quarter to interview graduates for jobs. I had my resumé, letters of recommendation from my professors, a 4.0 average in my classes, and a high score on the state teachers exam. I was ready to start my new career. All I needed was a job. When I walked into the interview with the person from Houston County, the first words out of her mouth were, "You are not black."

Here we go again. "No, I'm not."

"I'm sorry, we thought you were black. You have excellent test scores and recommendations, but we're here to hire the best black teachers we can find." They hired one of the young men who copied off my physics lab paper during my first quarter. I was the number one graduate, but I didn't get one offer from the job fair.

As I drove away from Northeast Alabama State College for the last time, I finally understood how many black people feel when they're qualified for a job but not given the opportunity because of the color of their skin.

CHAPTER 21

There were only two middle schools in Saint Clair County and there were no job openings for the next school year. I spent the summer sending my resumé to school systems within a fifty-mile radius. The HR directors had never heard of Troops to Teachers and didn't seem concerned with saving money.

I called principals in the surrounding counties, but I didn't get many interviews. The principals didn't care that the Troops to Teachers' program would pay seventy-five percent of my first year's salary. Principals didn't manage the salaries.

I had heard horror stories about the Birmingham city schools so I was reluctant to apply in Jefferson County but by August, with the start of school only two weeks away and not having heard from the small counties around home, I sent my resumé to Birmingham City Schools.

Four days after teachers reported to work in Birmingham, I got a call from Albert Bevins, a principal asking if I could come in for an interview. The Sixteenth Street Middle School, surrounded by a 10-foot fence topped by razor wire, looked more like a prison than a school. A guard at the gate took my name and logged who I was visiting.

Since Birmingham City School District didn't allow race to be placed on their applications Mr. Bevins didn't know that I was white. He assumed because I got my certification from Northeast State that I was black. The first words out of his mouth when I walked into his office were, "You're not black."

"What gave it away?"

Predictably, his next question was, "Why did you go to Northeast State?"

I had left my Paul Harvey cards at home, so I had to explain.

To his credit, he didn't dismiss me out of hand. He explained that he was looking for a teacher to teach seventh grade science. The seventh grade had two teams and since I went to Northeast State, he had thought I would fit in with the teachers on the team. Until he figured out I wasn't black.

Knowing my options were limited, I asked to meet the other team members and I followed him to the seventh-grade hall where he introduced me to the three team members. I got a cool reception with a clear message that they had established procedures and would expect me to follow them. They alluded to problems with the last science teacher, whom I later found out lasted only three days before quitting. In fact, they had run off two teachers in less than a year. The Social Studies teacher came right out and said that she had problems with white teachers. I assured her she wouldn't have a problem with me because I went to Northeast State, and everybody knows white folk don't go to Northeast State. School was starting in two days and Mr. Bevins was desperate for a science teacher, so he offered me the job.

The next morning, I called and accepted the offer. I drove over to Birmingham to the Central Office to fill out my employment paperwork. I told the HR director that I was in the Troops to Teachers program, but she had never heard of it and didn't seem interested. I spent the next day getting my classroom ready for students which included a poster listing the classroom rules. When the Social Studies teacher, Serena Clark, came by my room and saw the poster she told me to take it down. She informed me that as the team leader everything needed her approval and I had not gotten it.

"Why didn't you tell me yesterday?" I asked.

Glaring at me she said, "I didn't think the principal would hire you after the problems we've had with white teachers."

I decided this was a hill I'd stand on and my smart-ass response was, "I went to Northeast State, so I can't be white."

She didn't smile as she walked away.

I left my poster up and started working on my lesson plans for the first week.

My stomach was full of butterflies as I welcomed my first students to my homeroom class. I had my name written on the board. I introduced myself and a hand went up. "Is your name Mr. Tall Butt?" The class broke into hysterical laughter. Classroom management, where is a dirt clod when you need one? I ignored the question and started explaining the classroom rules. Another hand went up. "Hey Tall Butt, I gotta go pee."

At the middle school where I did my practice teaching, when a student asked to go to the restroom, the teacher gave the student a hall pass. However, this was a school in the "hood" and Ms. Clark clearly communicated that you didn't let anyone go to the restroom because they smoke dope, drop a cherry bomb down the commode, or walk off and don't come back.

The team had two restroom breaks at 10 AM and 1:30 PM where all four classes went to the restroom at the same time. Since I was the only male on the team it was my job to go into the boy's restroom and monitor behavior. One of the women would go into the girl's. The other two teachers kept an eye on behavior in the hallway. When all who needed to did their business, we walked back to the classrooms as a group. This had been a procedure that all classes followed for years and all the students who had been in the school for the sixth grade knew the restroom policy. My "I gotta go pee" student was testing the new teacher.

"Did you go to school here last year?" I asked her.

"Yeah," she muttered, not making eye contact.

"So, you know the restroom policy."

"I got to pee," she insisted, making eye contact this time. In the next second she stood up, squatted next to her desk, and peed on the floor. The class went wild. Damn! Where is a dirt clod when you need one? I called the office and explained what had happened and asked that a janitor come clean up the pee.

The names of my students were a challenge for me to pronounce as I called the roll for the first time. I was used to Bill, Fred, James,

Judy, Peggy, or Janice. There were no names like these names on my roll. I had a girl named Breanka who was at least seven months pregnant and only 13 years old. During a subsequent conference with her mother, she told me that she had Breanka when she was 13 and she was now going to be a grandmother before she turned 27. This was not the almost-all-white middle school where I did my practice teaching.

At lunch, I told the other team members about the girl peeing on the floor. Of course, they had already heard about it from the students. One of the teachers explained that the girl was nicknamed "Big Fat" and she had done the same thing the first day of school last year.

During the team's planning period I asked what discipline plan the team used and was informed that after three warnings the student was sent to the principal and would be assigned to the alternative class for the rest of the day.

"What do the students do in the alternative class?" I asked.

"Most of them sleep," a team member replied.

When I did my practice teaching we used positive reinforcement to get the students to behave in class. Every month they had a pizza party for the students who had two or less referrals. The pizza was donated to the school by Pizza Hut. Over the next few days, I made some phone calls. I called a colleague at my old middle-school and got the name of the regional manager for Pizza Hut. He gave me the name of the Pizza Hut regional manager in Birmingham. I called him and he gave me the name of the manager of the Pizza Hut about two miles from my school. I made an appointment with the manager and to my relief, she thought it was a great idea to give the students positive reinforcement to improve their behavior. She told me that she had attended my school.

When I brought the idea up to my team, Ms. Clark said it wouldn't work, "Nobody is going to give us free pizza." I explained that I had already talked to the Pizza Hut manager and she was going to provide the pizza.

"You got it because you're white, they wouldn't have given it to us if we had asked them," Social Studies said.

"The manager is black. She went to this school. She would have given you the same thing she agreed to give me," I countered.

"Bevins won't approve it," another team member interjected.

"Let's ask him," I said and headed for the principal's office.

After a brief discussion, Mr. Bevins approved the idea, but he wanted it for all the teams. I called the local Pizza Hut manager and explained the wrinkle. Unfortunately, she couldn't afford to provide free pizza for the whole school but was still willing to donate pizza for the seventh-grade teams.

"Thank you for your generous offer but I guess my positive reinforcement idea is dead," I said, disappointed.

My hopes for the plan were revived when she offered, "Let me call my regional manager and see if I can get two more stores to provide pizza for the sixth and eighth graders. I'll call you back tomorrow. Don't give up on your positive reinforcement idea just yet."

The next morning, I had a phone call. "Your idea lives. My regional manager talked to the district manager and Pizza Hut has adopted Sixteenth Street Middle School."

She gave me the contacts who would supply pizzas for the sixth and eighth grade teams. All we had to do was call them three days before the date we wanted the pizzas, and they would deliver at the time we requested.

I gave Mr. Bevins the good news that three local Pizza Huts had adopted Sixteenth Street Middle School and there would be pizza for all the teams. Now that the first hurdle had been eliminated, we got down to business. He wondered how the teams could keep up with the number of times a student had been referred to the office. I suggested his secretary keep a list for each grade and provide the names to the team leaders of the students who had over two referrals.

Bevins briefed the staff at the next staff meeting about a new positive reinforcement program that he was instituting. He informed the teachers that he had gotten Pizza Hut to adopt

Sixteenth Street Middle School and donate pizza for a pizza party for all the students who had two or less referrals per month. He went on to say that he had told the Superintendent about his idea and the Superintendent was thinking about adopting the idea system wide. I wasn't surprised that he was taking credit for the idea and using it for brownie points with the Superintendent. Politics is alive and well in school administration.

Still Social Studies was skeptical, "That might work in a mostly white school, but it won't work in a black school in the hood."

Our first party was planned for the end of September, and I volunteered to monitor the students who could not attend. Social Studies insisted that all students from our team should attend, because if we didn't allow all of them, the bad actors would act up even more. She refused to recognize that by doing so, it would defeat the purpose of the program by rewarding students for bad behavior and removing the incentive to behave. Referrals would not go down and she could then claim my idea didn't work.

She was passive-aggressive, but she wasn't politically savvy. She didn't realize that the idea was now Bevins', and he needed the referrals to go down so he could get his brownie points from the Superintendent.

Serena's sabotage campaign worked, and the other team leaders sent all their students to the party. Referrals didn't go down and Mr. Bevins was not a happy camper. He called me into his office to discuss why referrals were as high or higher than they had been before the program.

I explained that all the team leaders were not supporting the program and without a commitment from everyone the plan was destined to fail.

At the monthly staff meeting, he turned the tables. He announced a change in policy. From that point forward, he would personally be monitoring the number of referrals from each teacher and excessive referrals would reflect on annual evaluations. He informed us he expected teachers to solve discipline problems in the classroom and he set a limit of not more than two students per teacher be referred to the office per week.

The next day Social Studies informed our team that we would employ a zero-tolerance policy. No student who had any referrals would get to go to the party. She was determined to get a good evaluation.

During homeroom I explained to my students that there were no more free passes. From now on they had to behave, or they would have to work while the respectful students ate pizza and listened to music.

Some of the students doubted me, but the party at the end of October made believers out of them.

CHAPTER 22

When I gave my first test a group of students earned a grade of 100. I found it suspect because they never paid attention in class, never took notes, and I never saw them with a textbook. I assumed one of them must have stolen my answer sheet. At the end of class, I asked one of the better students to stay for a few minutes.

"Nayasha, have you heard anyone talking about cheating on the test?"

Being a good student in this school singled one out, but not in a positive way, and I could tell she was reluctant to answer knowing it could ostracize her even further with her peers.

"Why should others cheat to get their grade when you've worked hard to earn yours?" I prodded.

Eventually her moral compass swung in the right direction, and she told me the name of the boy who had stolen my answer sheet. For the next test, I employed my trick from physics class at Northeast State. I left the sheet with wrong answers inside the science book on my desk three days before the test. My plan was to watch the boy and catch him red handed, but I never saw him go near my desk.

When I graded the test the group who made 100 on the last test all scored a 46. They had given the wrong answers from my false answer sheet. When I gave the tests back, the boy who Nayasha told me had stolen the answers raised his hand and said I had made a mistake grading his paper. It was déjà vu all over again.

"No, there was no mistake on my part. Apparently one of you found an answer sheet on my desk and thought it was for this test."

Students started yelling that they wanted their money back. They had paid the boy for the answers. Obviously, I told the perpetrator to stay after class.

With an air of defiance, he stood in front of my desk waiting to see what I was going to do.

"So, Dante. If you were me, what would you do about this?" I began.

"Y'all gonna do whatever," he mumbled.

I got up and took a seat at one of the student desks in the front row and told him to sit down.

"You really didn't give me much choice, Dante. You stole answers to a test and took money from other students."

"Tall Butt, that's the way things work in our world."

"Dante don't disrespect me. You know my name and how you should address a teacher. This street act doesn't get you anywhere in the classroom. You'll find out sooner or later, the easy way or the hard way, when the act works and when it doesn't."

He said nothing and picked at the cuticle on his thumb.

"Look, I'm going to give you a choice. The consequences of your actions are going to be entirely in your hands. I either send you to the office with a referral or you tell me how you stole the answer sheet. I never saw you go near my desk."

He smiled slyly, "It's bothern' I got over on you when you was tryin' to trap me, not that we cheat."

"Not true, Dante. I care that you cheated because if you don't learn, life's going to get harder for you and it's my job to teach you what you need to know. Look, do you want your mom to be proud of you or ashamed? Do you want to be proud of yourself? Do you know how good it feels to accomplish something you never were able to do before?"

We sat quietly for a few minutes as his bravado slipped away. "I don't want my mom to be ashamed," he said. "My brother's on the street and does shit that's gonna get him put away. Nothin' she can do about him. I hear her talkin' to her friends and I hear her cryin' sometimes."

"Then give her something to be proud of. Be a man and face the music for what you did and start thinking about consequences before you act. For this, you miss a pizza party. You keep going down this road and you'll end up like your brother."

It's surprising how losing a pizza party loosened a twelve-year-old's tongue.

"I didn't go near your desk, Mr. Talbert. Samuel, the night janitor, steals the answer sheets from all the classes, makes copies and puts them back. There's one person in each class he sells to and then we sell them to the other students. I'm sorry, it's just so hard tryin' to learn this stuff sometimes, and buyin' the answers is easy."

"I appreciate you being honest, Dante. We're going to call this a lesson learned, okay? No more cheating. You know, I think Nayasha might be willing to stay after school to help you if you need it."

His eyes lit up with the idea of spending some time with a cute girl who had brains. "That's a deal, Mr. Talbert, and I could use some extra help."

After quietly asking around I discovered the janitor had a sweet deal not only selling answers to tests but weed as well. I took my information to Mr. Bevins, only to be told that I couldn't believe Dante. Nothing I said could convince him Dante was telling the truth. Other teachers had suspected all along what was going on but said nothing. It was discouraging that no one seemed to care that these kids were learning the wrong lessons.

Much later I found out that the janitor was Bevins' first cousin and I suspect he was probably in on the scheme which would explain the Rolex watch he wore and the top-of-the-line BMW he drove.

At the end of the first six weeks, we turned our grades in to the team leaders before we recorded them on the students' report cards. More than half my students had failing grades. They didn't turn in assignments, didn't take notes even after I had a class on note taking, didn't bring their textbook to class and flunked the tests. I had called their parents and asked for parent-teacher conferences, but only two parents were interested enough to show up.

Some of the students lived in foster homes. One woman had eight foster kids who went to our school. The state paid her for each child in her care. I didn't know if she had a generous heart, whether the extra money helped make ends meet, or if it was a profit-making business, and it wasn't my place to judge. But I paid extra attention to the foster kids in my class and was alert for any signs of neglect or abuse.

Before report cards were handed out, I reminded the students that they would fail and must repeat the grade if they didn't study and pass. They laughed. One boy bragged that he had never opened a book and always passed and most of the others agreed. Based on my evaluation, he read on a kindergarten level.

Ms. Clark reviewed my grades and returned them without comment. I printed them and sent them to the front office, whereupon I got a call to come to the principal's office.

Mr. Bevins was clearly upset when I walked into his office. "Why didn't you follow the instructions that Serena gave you?"

Confused, I asked, "What do you mean?"

"She told you that the lowest grade you could give is 60."

"She never told me that," I protested.

"Are you calling her a liar?"

"I am saying that she never told me that."

"I just spoke to her, and she said that you don't follow her instructions. Did you refuse to take down a poster that she had not approved?"

"The poster lists my classroom rules, and all the other classrooms have their rules posted."

"Look, Talbert, you might have been a full colonel in the Air Force but here you'll follow the orders given to you by your team leader and by me. Go change the grades!"

"Sir, yes sir," I said sarcastically, turned on my heal, and left his office.

It was now clear why the last two science teachers had quit. Not only was there a lack of interest in seeing the students succeed, but Serena Clark also didn't want white teachers on her team. During the planning period I walked into her classroom and asked her if we could talk. I closed the door and took a seat at a student desk.

"Ms. Clark, I'm not your enemy, I'm your peer teacher who wants to work with you to instruct these students. If we are going to be team members we must work together, not against each other. It's clear you dislike me. Is it because I'm white?"

She looked as if I had slapped her in the face and without hesitation, she said, "Do you really want to know why I don't like whites, Mr. Talbert?"

"What I would like is to have a better understanding of why we can't work together," I said sincerely.

Serena signed heavily and walked to the window. With her back to me she began, "When I was a senior in high school my all-black school was closed, and we were bussed to the white high school. I was number one in my class, ready to be valedictorian at graduation, before I was bussed to that white school. Do you know what it feels like to be ostracized, yelled at, called names, and spat on, Mr. Talbert?"

"No, Ms. Clark, I don't, not like that, but I've felt the sting of racism. I was the only white person at Northeast State."

She gave no indication that she'd heard me.

"We were treated like we had a contagious disease. That last year of high school was hell and I couldn't wait to graduate. I had been accepted at Fort Valley State College in Georgia where I'd be back in an all-black school. I met my husband there and even with us both earning degrees, we just never measured up to your white world's standards. Just this year, my husband was passed over for a promotion he earned. His boss gave the position to his white buddy."

She turned back to face me and said, "So, Mr. Talbert, yes I resent the fact that a white person comes into our school, into our community, and thinks they know what's best for us, for our children." With that she crossed the room and opened the door. Our conversation was clearly over.

I now had a better understanding of what made Serena Clark tick, but it didn't make my situation any better. I felt like I was beating my head against a brick wall. No one cared if the students learned anything, give them a 60, pass them on up the line until they dropped out. Every morning when I drove through the gate with the razor wire fence, I wondered what difference it made if I taught or if I just let the students sleep. They would get a 60 for doing nothing and be promoted to the eighth grade. No one seemed to care where the students were going, they kept saying, "You don't understand where they come from." I knew where they were going if the system kept letting them do nothing then passing them to the next grade.

During the first week of December, we had a fire drill and all the students had to assemble in the parking lot while the fire department was in the school. When we were back inside, one of the teachers told me Big Fat had hit my truck with her fist and put a dent in the door. I reported it Mr. Bevins who said, "What do you want me to do? Report it to your insurance."

Frustrated, I explained, "I have a $500 deductible. Is the school going to reimburse me for that? Are you going to discipline Big Fat?"

"The answer to your first question is no and you didn't see her do it, so the answer to your second question is no."

I gave him the name of the teacher who witnessed the incident and he agreed to investigate. Two weeks later he still had not talked to the witness and he had not disciplined Big Fat.

Just before the end of the semester Big Fat was in my class reading a gossip magazine, not paying any attention to what I was teaching. I walked back to her desk, picked up her magazine and told her she would get it back at the end of class. She jumped up and yelled, "You four-eyed motherfucker, give me back my magazine or I'll whip your ass."

I paged the security officer assigned to the school and told him to remove her from my class. I wrote up the incident and sent it to the office. Not five minutes later Big Fat was back in my class and told me Bevins said to give her magazine back. I told her she would get it back at the end of class.

"I'll cut you, you don't give it back to me now!" she screeched. I called security again and had her taken out of class. I wrote up the incident and sent it to the office. Within ten minutes, she was back from the office with a note from Bevins to me to give her the magazine.

Defeated, I handed her the magazine. As she tore it from my hand she said menacingly, "I may still cut you after school."

During my planning period I went to see Mr. Bevins and asked him if he was going to discipline Big Fat. He said he had talked to her. I told him that I felt her behavior warranted something more than a talking to. To my surprise, he told me that the exchange was my fault for taking her magazine and that he was going to write me up for poor class management.

"Save your time, Bevins, I quit," I said angrily.

His only reply was, "Give me your resignation in writing."

I typed up my resignation letter and, on my way out at the end of the day, I handed it to the secretary. That December afternoon I drove through the gate of Sixteenth Street Middle School for the last time. Four days later Bevins called me and asked if I would come back. He offered to take Big Fat out of my class. I told him I'd think about it. That afternoon, to my surprise, Serena Clark also called and explained that the students wanted me to come back. Having given it some thought between phone calls from Bevins and Clark, I declined. It would be better if they hired a black teacher.

Rolling pills didn't seem so bad compared to teaching middle school. If all else failed, maybe I could get a job as a greeter at Walmart, anything but a middle school teacher.

CHAPTER 23

By 1994 I knew I didn't want to continue running my drug store and I had taught my last class in Middle School. A phone call from HAT and Stephanie helped me decide what I wanted to do with the rest of my life.

"Hey Mom and Dad, how are things?" HAT's voice echoed from feedback over the phone's speaker.

"Just fine, son. We're looking forward to the end of this miserable winter. How are things with you?"

"Enjoying the green grass and sunshine. Why don't you guys plan on a short trip and get your batteries recharged?"

"That sounds inviting, we'll give it some thought. Anything else going on in your lives."

"Well, let me think. Steph, what else is going on?"

"Oh, don't be a tease HAT," Stephanie interjected and took over the conversation. "We got great news yesterday. You'll need to plan a trip down at the end of the summer to welcome your first grandchild. I'm due in August."

The decibel level of Sue's joyful scream almost busted my eardrum.

After congratulating HAT and Stephanie and promising to get down for a visit sooner rather than later, Sue and I toasted the coming of our family's first baby in a generation over hot toddies in front of the fire and talked about the future.

Coincidently, a national pharmacy chain had approached me a few weeks before about buying the drug store. Sue thought the universe was sending us a message. I called them and told them to write the check.

Sue and I put the cabin up for sale and booked a moving company to move all our belongings to Florida. We flew down to Lakeland and made an offer on a house just up the street from HAT and Stephanie in Eagles Landing. We closed on the house the 11th of February and moved in the following day. As we rode through the gate into Eagles Landing, I noticed a trapeze in the side yard of the first house.

"Sue, that looks like what they use in a circus. I wonder who lives there."

When we arrived at our new home the moving van was only a few minutes behind us. We got the doors unlocked and the movers began to unload boxes and furniture. Sue was inside supervising, and I was standing outside in the driveway when the next-door neighbor walked over to welcome us to the neighborhood. I introduced myself and to my surprise, he said, "I thought that was you. I'm Bill Alden, you probably don't remember me, but I knew you as Cadet Major Talbert back at Auburn. You were two years ahead of me and you were my Squadron Commander in AFROTC."

"I can't believe that you recognized me after all these years. It's been almost thirty years."

"When I first saw you standing here, I thought I knew you from somewhere. When you told me your name it clicked. It's good to have another Auburn man in the neighborhood. I've been outnumbered by Gators and Seminoles. If there is anything we can do to help you get settled just let us know."

"Thanks very much, but our son lives down the street on the lake, so I'll bother him first," I said smiling, "Let's catch up later, I need to let my son know that we arrived."

For Christmas HAT had presented Sue and I with matching Nokia 2110 mobile phones. He had programmed his and Stephanie's numbers in the memory and I pressed '2' for Stephanie.

"Hello Steph, we're here. They're unloading our furniture."

"Hi Robert, we'll be down in a few minutes. I'll help Sue get unpacked and HAT can help you get the furniture arranged just the way she wants it."

A few minutes later the '52 Ford drove into the driveway. After hugs, we joined Sue in the house amidst a mountain of boxes and furniture. HAT and I started by carrying chairs to place them around the dining table. "Have you met your neighbor Bill?" HAT asked as we worked.

"Yes, just before you arrived. An Auburn alum. He was in my AFROTC squadron."

"You know Dad, the more I see of the world, the more I'm reminded how small it really is," HAT observed, "Bill has the largest CPA firm in Lakeland with a number of the Tigers baseball players as clients."

As we worked, I asked, "What's with the trapeze in the yard of the first house as you come into the neighborhood?"

Laughing, HAT explained, "That's where The Great Zelda Santinni lives. She's a featured act with the Ringling Brothers Circus. Last August, while performing in Charlotte, she took a bad fall and has been recovering at home. When she began practicing again, the trapeze went up. Sarasota is the circus' winter home. They get back on the road at the end of the month and I suppose she'll join them."

We started slicing boxes open. "Zelda's husband is Boris Brotski, an MMA fighter in the UFC. He's a local hero. Played at Lakeland High School was All American at the University of Tampa back when they had a football team and was drafted in the first round by the Raiders. He looks like a steroid freak. He showed up to the HOA annual meeting in January and got so drunk I had to drive him home. This neighborhood has some interesting characters."

The next few weeks were taken up with getting the house in order. When the bills began to arrive at the end of the month, I took stock of our financial situation. Our military retirement from the reserves wouldn't kick in until our sixtieth birthdays and we were more than a decade away from being able to draw Social

Security at 62. The profits from the sale of the drug store were invested to cover our retirement and would only be used for emergencies. We needed health insurance so unless we wanted to quickly deplete our savings, we needed to get jobs. Sue applied at the hospital in Bartow and at Lakeland Regional Medical Center. There were two national drug store chains within a mile of our subdivision, so I put in applications and at the hospital in Bartow.

Sue got a call from the Bartow hospital. They had a night shift supervisor's position open. She would work three twelve-hour shifts and be paid for 40 hours. The next day Lakeland Regional called and wanted to interview her for a med/surg unit position on the day shift, on weekends. The money was better at Regional, so she took the job when they made an offer. A week later the Walgreens district manager called and asked me to come in for an interview. He had a part-time position at the store near our house. My hours would be Friday, Saturday, and Sunday from 9 AM to 7 PM, filling in on other days if a pharmacist was out. If a full-time position came open, I would be moved into it.

Between the two jobs and our liquid savings we could live comfortably for the next nine years until our reserve retirement kicked in.

One Saturday afternoon I was talking to a customer who boasted that he had found the perfect part-time job towing travel trailers up north.

"People from up north buy trailers in Florida because they are cheaper here. I use my truck; the dealer pays for my fuel and gives me $150 per diem and $2,000 per trip. Most of my deliveries are to Atlanta, Charlotte, Nashville, or Birmingham."

"Do they need any more drivers?" I asked.

"As a matter of fact, they do. There is one catch, they want husband and wife teams," he explained.

"My wife and I work on the weekends, so we have four days open. Where do I apply?"

"Dave's Camper Sales in Winter Haven. Tell Dave, Bud sent you."

"Thanks, I'll do that."

Monday morning, Sue and I drove over to Dave's Camper Sales. It wasn't a big RV dealership. They had maybe twenty trailers and three old class-A motorhomes. The place looked rather run down and the small office was a temporary metal building. A middle-aged woman who looked as if she might be in her fifties, with dyed red hair and a cigarette hanging on her lip, sat behind a desk.

"Good morning," I said congenially, "We'd like to see Dave about a driving job. Bud sent us,"

"You got an appointment?" she asked in a husky voice.

"No, I'm sorry, we don't. We can make one if Dave isn't available."

"He's not here right now. He should be back in a few minutes if you want to wait."

"Thanks, we'll wait. Do you mind if we look at the RVs?" I asked.

"Help yourselves. Some of them are locked, ready for shipment, so you can't get inside them."

I noticed that four trailers had sold signs on them. As we stepped out of one of the old class-As, a late-model Mercedes pulled into the parking lot and a large man got out. He skin was the color of a latte, he had slicked-back black hair, a gold chain around his neck, and a diamond pinky ring. He walked into the office and within minutes came out and walked to where we were looking at a small popup.

Holding a big cigar between his teeth, he introduced himself as Dave. "Babs said that Bud sent you about a driving job. Is that your truck?"

"Yes, it is. I'm Robert Talbert and this is my wife, Sue."

"Have you ever pulled a travel trailer before?" he asked.

"No, but I've pulled a large bass boat."

"Okay. Do you object to me installing a fifth-wheel hitch on your pickup?"

"Not if you are paying for it," I said.

"Good. You get $2,000 plus $150 per diem per trip. I pay you half in cash the day you leave plus your per diem. I'll fill up your tank when you depart and when you return. You'll be paid $1,000 in cash when you deliver the trailer. Normally the dealer on the other end will fill up your tank before you leave his shop, but not always.

This time of the year I ship a lot of RVs north. Dealers up north call me and tell me what kind of RV their customers want and if I don't have it in inventory, I usually can find something at the RV auction. You would be surprised how many people come to Florida in the winter with their RVs and drop dead or get sick and can't drive them back north. The RV auction is full of them this time of the year and they sell at an exceptionally low price compared to what they sell for up north. Any chance you could make a trip tomorrow? I have a trailer that needs to be delivered to Oxford, Alabama. That's up near Birmingham."

I looked at Sue and she nodded, "That works for us. We know that area well, we just moved from that area in February."

"Be here at seven in the morning. You need to deliver the trailer by 6 PM They close at 6:30, so if you have a problem and can't make it before closing time, call them and let them know. Drive at the speed limit. I don't pay speeding tickets."

It seemed strange that we didn't have to fill out any employment paperwork. Since we would be paid in cash, I assumed that everything was off the books.

Tuesday morning, we got on the road at 7:30 pulling a 32-foot tag-along. It was the first time I had towed a large trailer, so I had some trepidation but did okay until we got to I-75. The first time a large 18-wheeler passed me I could feel the wind buffeting the truck. It was white knuckle time. I dropped my speed down and hugged the right lane. This helped and after a while I wasn't squeezing the steering wheel. We pulled into the dealer in Oxford five minutes before six and were told to pull the trailer around to the service area. The dealer, who looked like he could be a close relative to Dave, signed our paperwork, paid us in cash, and gave us $100 for gas. We checked into the Holiday Inn, ate dinner, and went to bed early. We were on the road by 6 AM and got back to Winter Haven by four. Dave took the signed paperwork, filled up our truck, and asked if we could make a run the following week to deliver a trailer to Atlanta.

"Put us down for it," I said.

"Okay, unless I call you, be here at 7 AM Tuesday."

On April 1ˢᵗ, HAT left for Detroit to begin a new season and Stephanie stayed in Lakeland to finish the school year. In June, she flew up to join HAT in Detroit. In late July, she returned to Lakeland because she couldn't travel after the first of August.

On the 11ᵗʰ of August, the Major League Baseball Players Association called for a strike because the owners were attempting to install a salary cap and the last labor agreement had expired at the end of December. The owners were not negotiating in good faith. They wanted to break the player's union. Fifty games and the World Series were canceled. HAT returned to Lakeland to wait for the birth of their first child.

"Robert. Wake up, the phone is ringing," Sue said nudging me in the ribs.

With eyes barely open, I fumbled for the phone on my side of the bed and croaked, "Hello."

"Dad, we're leaving for the hospital," HAT said, his voice betrayed none of the adrenaline I knew he had to be feeling.

The time had come, the reason why we sold out and moved to Florida was happening. We were about to become grandparents.

Stephanie's parents had their plane on standby, so they were in the air before HAT and Stephanie got to the hospital. HAT went back to the delivery room with Stephanie while we paced in the waiting room. Two and a half hours after they got the call, Harriet and Frank walked in.

"Has she delivered yet?" Harriet asked anxiously.

"No, I'm beginning to think it's a false alarm," I said.

"Robert, this is her first child, and they always take longer to deliver. She's only been in labor for three hours. I was in labor for four hours with HAT," Sue said.

"Frank, be a dear and go call The Terrace Hotel and reserve a suite. Make sure it faces the lake and is on the top floor."

"Yes dear," Frank answered dutifully, excusing himself to make the arrangements.

After five hours of labor, on August 19, 1994, Elisabeth Anne Talbert made her grand entrance into the world and took over my life. I was no longer Right Hand. I was now Paw-Paw and Sue became Maw-Maw.

When HAT and Stephanie brought Elisabeth Anne home, Frank and Harriet checked out of The Terrace Hotel and moved into the guest room. Harriet informed everyone that she planned to stay for a month to help Stephanie with the baby. Frank laughed at the idea, telling us he didn't know how she could help with a baby because she had never changed a diaper in her life.

Harriet gave Frank his marching orders, "Go home and manage the foundry and I'll hire a nanny for Elisabeth."

CHAPTER 24

The baseball owners continued to play hard ball for six months. Thanksgiving and Christmas passed and 1995 arrived with the strike not settled. The date for catchers and pitchers to report to spring training passed without a new contract. As negotiations continued, the owners decided to withhold $7.8 million that they were required to pay into the players' pension and benefit plans per the previous agreement. In addition, owners had illegally withdrawn money from the retirement fund in the past. They were determined to break the union and decided to play the season with replacement players that came from independent leagues and semi-pro teams.

The TV network big shots were concerned about the quality of the replacement players and their effect on ratings. They were putting pressure on the owners to settle the strike, but the good-old-boy owners dug in their heels.

Owners longed for the time before free agency when players were subject to reserve clauses in contracts and owners could dictate who played and how much players got paid. During those years players were essentially indentured servants. If owners failed to make contractually-obligated payments and a player didn't like it, he could go get a job in a factory.

When free agency came about, the owners colluded to keep the salaries low. Even the best free-agent players could not find a team that would give them a contract, so they had to sign with their old team at the salary dictated by the team. Players sued, the owners lost, and owners were required to pay $280,000,000 in damages to the players.

The morning the scab players showed up at Tiger Town for spring training players picketed the entrances where police and deputy sheriffs were posted to ensure that no violence took place. Some of the fans supported the players, but most felt the players were overpaid prima donnas. The owners controlled a powerful propaganda machine.

The owners continuously reported the average player salary as almost $1.1 million and claimed they were going broke because of the high salaries. What they didn't tell the public was that the average was skewed because of a few exceedingly high contracts. The median salary was only $339,500. Half the players made less than $339,000. Many of the players made the minimum of $109,000. It was hard to convince someone who made $27,845, the annual average pay in 1995, that the ball players were underpaid.

The players union brought a suit in federal court to stop the owners from using replacement players. Judge Sonia Sotomayer of the U.S. District Court of New York issued a preliminary injunction against the owners on March 31st prohibiting them from using replacement players. This brought the owners back to the negotiating table and on April 2nd the players agreed to begin play for the 1995 season, ending the strike. Normally spring training lasts six or seven weeks but after a three-week spring training the regular season started on April 26, 1995.

The first of March, Tony Perez had flown up from his home in Puerto Rico and moved into HAT's guest room. They had always worked out together before the reporting date for pitchers and catchers at Tiger Town but this year they had been locked out. The baseball coach at Florida Southern College let them use the college diamond in the morning and they helped coach the FSC team in the afternoon. When the season began HAT and Tony were ahead of most of the other players. Their extra work paid off because they both made the All-Star team.

Throughout the summer we continued to pull trailers up to Atlanta and Oxford. I thought the trips would drop off, but they continued every week. The guy who told me about the job came by the pharmacy and told me he was making a trip up to Charleston every week. The used RV trailer business was booming.

At the end of August, Sue and I flew up to Washington D.C. for George Daniel's retirement ceremony from the Air Force and stayed in the same hotel with JB and Selma. George had done very well and retired as a Brigadier General. He was going to work for one of the biggest law firms in D.C. I never thought, back at Auburn when George was spending most of his time drinking at a beer joint called the Library, that someday he would retire as a BG and be a lawyer at a major law firm. The three musketeers had a great reunion.

In September, after we dropped off a trailer in Oxford, we met old friends for dinner, and they mentioned that one of their retired friends from church was delivering trailers for Cheaha RV. That was the dealer in Oxford where we made deliveries. "He makes a delivery to Memphis about every other Wednesday."

As we drove back to the motel after dinner, I asked Sue if she thought it strange that a small RV dealer in Oxford was selling trailers to people in Memphis.

"No stranger than us delivering a trailer to Oxford every two weeks," she answered.

"Something's not right. I don't know what it is, but something's not right."

Wednesday morning rather than head for Florida first thing. I drove past Cheaha RV and parked in the lot of a strip mall just down the road. At 7:30 a red Ford F-150® pulling the very same trailer we had delivered Tuesday afternoon drove past us headed towards the west bound I-20 on-ramp.

Two weeks later we dropped off a trailer at Cheaha RV. Wednesday morning, I parked and waited to see if the red Ford came past with the trailer we had delivered. Right on time the red Ford F-150® went past pulling the trailer that we had delivered.

"Sue this can't be coincidental, something is rotten in Denmark."

The next week we delivered a trailer to Atlanta and the next morning I waited down the road to see if the trailer we had delivered was being moved to another destination. After waiting for two hours, we hadn't seen our trailer go past. I slowed down as we drove past the RV dealer and there on the front row was the trailer that we had delivered.

"Do you still think something is rotten in Denmark?" Sue asked.

The next two trips to Oxford the red F-150® didn't show up and I had to admit that maybe it was my wild imagination. But I couldn't shake the feeling that something was wrong. As we were on our way to pick up our next delivery, I told Sue I still had reservations about our deliveries to Cheaha RV.

I wanted to get a look inside the trailers that we delivered but they were sealed. The windows were tinted so you couldn't see inside, and Dave had been very explicit that we were not to open any of the trailers.

On the next trip to Oxford, we were pulling a 32-foot tag-along. A trailer that length should have an unloaded vehicle weight (UVW) of about 7,000 pounds. There is a truck stop south of Ocala on I-75 that has a truck scale, so I decided to weigh the trailer. While Sue went to use the facilities, I paid $10 and pulled the trailer up on the scale. The scale showed that the trailer weighed 10,000 pounds. That came close to the gross axle weight rate, the weight the trailer can safely support. When Sue came back, I didn't mention that I had weighed the trailer. Wednesday morning, I waited for the red Ford F-150®. Right on time, at 7:30, it rolled past heading for the west bound I-20 on-ramp. Now, there was no doubt in my mind that we had unwittingly become part of something nefarious, but I didn't know what.

I was covering for another pharmacist on Thursday morning, debating who I should call about my trailer-delivery concerns when none other than Gill Maxwell walked into Walgreens.

"Well, I'll be. If it's not Right Hand Talbert!" Gill exclaimed when he saw me. Knowing that nothing about encounters with Gill could be a coincidence, I was speechless.

I asked a pharm tech to cover me for a few minutes and came out from behind the counter. Shaking his hand I asked, "What are you doing in these parts? Do you have another trip for us?"

"No, no. I'm not down here on business, I'm here visiting a friend and my allergies are giving me fits, so I came in to get something to stop the watery eyes and stuffed-up nose. My friend lives just down the road. How's Sue?"

Still unconvinced of this being a chance encounter, I went along with the small talk, "Sue's great. We're grandparents. HAT and Stephanie had a baby girl. Follow me, Allegra's on aisle 3. That should take care of your symptoms."

"Congratulations on the baby. Time sure flies by, doesn't it?"

As Gill picked up a few more sundries to help with his 'allergies' I asked, "So, who's this friend of yours who lives just down the road?"

"You know her. She comes in and picks up her parents' prescriptions. She lives in that big house with the guitar-shaped swimming pool," he said with a smirk.

"Sweet Jesus, you've got to be kidding. Jean? Your 'friend' is Jean Auburndale? How the hell did that happen?" I had that feeling, which seemed to always coincide with encounters with Gill, of being in an alternate universe.

"See, you're smarter than you think. I slipped her my card before I made my sudden exit from Sloppy Joe's, and she called."

"Which card? Is it the Gill Maxwell card or the Art Nathanson card, or someone I haven't met yet?"

A few customers were in line at the pharmacy, so I had to get this encounter over with.

"It's the personal Gill card," he said as he fished in his pocket and handed me one. "I'm officially retired from my former occupation. Sometimes I travel with Jean when she has a gig, sometimes we spend some time in the Bahamas where I have a condo. Just living the good life."

I still didn't believe him, but I realized that either the federal government knew about my part-time job, or fate had manifested the one person who could help me with my dilemma. Either way, I needed Gill's help.

"I have something that I need your advice on," I said as Gill paid for his purchases, "I get out of here at seven. Can we meet?"

"Sure, how about Black 'n Brew at 7:30?" Gill said, smirking again.

I called Sue and told her I'd be late. She had plans to have dinner with Stephanie and Elisabeth, so she didn't mind. When I got to the coffee shop, I ordered a coffee and a freshly baked Danish, found a seat, and waited for Gill to arrive. By this time, I was convinced that an illicit enterprise was using unsuspecting retired folks to transport something illegal; guns, drugs, I didn't know what.

One kilo of cocaine weighs 2.2 pounds so a trailer could carry at least 1,360 kilos of cocaine or some other illegal drug. Guns are heavier so the haul wouldn't be as large but could be as lucrative.

Gill arrived, placed an order, and joined me at my table. I got right to the point and told him about my suspicions and about weighing the trailer. "So, come clean with me, Gill. Have you been watching us make these deliveries? Am I involved in this because you set us up with this part-time opportunity?"

"Robert, I'm retired. Our bumping into each other is just one of those fickle finger of fate encounters. But I agree with you, something is going on. Let me call a friend at DEA in the southern district of Florida. He used to be with the company before he moved over to DEA. He'll know what you should do."

The next morning at 7:30 my doorbell rang, and I opened it to two imposing men in dark suits.

"Good morning Mr. Talbert, I'm Special Agent Ingram of the FBI and this is Special Agent Matthews. We're here in response to a call we received last evening. May we come in?"

I hadn't mentioned anything to Sue about my meeting with Gill. From the look of concern on her face I knew she thought we were in some kind of trouble, given my suspicions about the travel-trailer deliveries.

Sue offered coffee which the agents declined, and we settled in around the dining room table. Agents Ingram and Matthews asked specific questions and recorded every detail of my answers about our trailer delivery job. I gave them the scale report which showed the weight of the trailer. When it was apparent there was nothing more to add, Sue asked, "Gentlemen, are we in some kind of trouble?"

They assured us we weren't, thanked us for our cooperation and told us to continue to deliver the trailers, but weigh each one and send the scale reports to the email address on the card Agent Ingram offered.

"Don't talk to anyone about this. We'll be in contact."

A month after the visit from the FBI, we arrived at Dave's RV to pick up a trailer and Dave wasn't there. Babs said he had called, and our trip was canceled because he had a problem at his ranch last night and couldn't get the trailer ready for delivery.

"Where's the ranch?" I asked casually.

"Oh, he has a 2,000-acre cattle ranch on the other side of Lake Wales," she answered.

When we got home, I called Special Agent Ingram and passed on the information about Dave's ranch.

For the next two months, I weighed every trailer. If asked, my explanation would be I was doing it to ensure that we were within the tow capacity of our truck. I didn't do any more surveillance of the red F-150®.

The week before Thanksgiving 1995, on Tuesday morning, Sue and I drove over to Dave's RV expecting to pick up a trailer for Oxford. As we approached Dave's, the street was blocked by Sheriff's cars, and I could see the flashing blue lights in the parking lot.

"Sorry folks, but you'll have to make a U-turn and go back to the corner. You can drive over one block and take 17th Street to get around the roadblock."

"What's going on officer?" Sue asked.

"I'm sorry, but I'm not at liberty to say. Please move on."

I made the U-turn and headed back to the house.

Tuesday night, our local sheriff, who loved seeing his mug on TV, was breaking news on all the Tampa and Orlando stations reporting on a joint task force with the FBI, DEA, and local law enforcement in twelve states which busted the largest cocaine distribution ring in the United States.

I turned up the volume, "A drug cartel in Columbia took a major hit today. Planes loaded with cocaine flew from an island in the Bahamas, stayed beneath the radar, and landed on a grass strip on a cattle ranch east of Lake Wales," the sheriff began.

"The cocaine was transferred to travel trailers and unsuspecting retired couples transported it all over the Eastern United States. The cartel had bought mom and pop RV dealers across the East coast and established their drug distribution network. Court records showed that the properties had been bought two years ago by RV Wholesalers LLC. We have pictures of planes landing on the ranch and cocaine being transferred to the travel trailers by three men."

The Sheriff continued, "Search warrants were issued, and we've impounded trailers in Oxford, Alabama, Atlanta, Memphis, Saint Louis, Charlotte, and Nashville. Over 50 people were arrested this morning with more arrests expected as the investigation continues. The United States government has taken custody of all the RV dealerships and the cattle ranch outside of Lake Wales along with an airplane."

Sue was in disbelief about the scope of the operation and that we had been transporting cocaine. "Do you think we will be arrested, Right?"

Listening carefully to the details in the press briefing, mentions of "Columbia", "Bahamas" confirmed my suspicions that my coincidental encounter with Gill was anything but. What I was still wondering about was his relationship with Jean.

"Right, what do you think, are we in trouble?" Sue repeated.

I knew we weren't, and I did my best to reassure her, "We may have to testify, but we've cooperated with the investigation, and they said we were 'unsuspecting retirees' so I don't think they'll be arresting us."

"Do you think the cartel will find out we were helping with the investigation and try to get revenge?" Sue persisted.

She had a valid point there. The cartels were dangerous, had tenacles everywhere and this was a big operation that was taken down. "I don't think they will, but let's have a security system installed just in case."

Later that day, Gill called and asked if we'd seen the news from our sheriff. When I told him we had, and that I was trusting my gut and didn't believe our reunion was coincidental, he just chuckled.

I also told him Sue was concerned for our safety, and he offered to arrange for installation of a security system that exceeded anything an average homeowner could acquire. I wasn't sure if that was meant to make me feel safer or implied the level of danger one was in if they found themselves in the crosshairs of a drug cartel.

As the prosecution of the cocaine-smuggling ring played out we learned that a house in our neighborhood had been owned by the lawyer who had set up RV Wholesalers LLC, the front for all the RV dealers across the Southeast. The lawyer had come into a large windfall, sold the house in Eagles Landing, and bought a house inside a private walled compound on one hundred-fifty acres on Lake Hancock.

That lawyer should have hired Gill to install a security system because two weeks after Dave, who was really Jose Hernandez an illegal from Columbia, was sent to the Federal maximum-security prison in Colorado for fifty years, someone broke into the lawyer's compound and killed him and his family.

The same sheriff, who ran unopposed in every election cycle, was on TV again. He explained the murders appeared to be a professional assassination carried out by a team who arrived and departed by helicopter.

While the arrests, convictions and confiscation of the cartel's property made for big headlines and opportunities for law enforcement to get 15 minutes of fame, it didn't stop the flow of illegal drugs coming into the United States. They were back in business the day after the first arrests.

CHAPTER 25

I found working for a chain much easier than running my own store. I worked nine to five, had a 401K, health insurance, sick leave, got three weeks' vacation, and someone else had the headaches of managing the store. At the end of 1995 I was offered, and accepted, a full-time pharmacist position with Walgreens.

While pharmacy work was routine and sometimes monotonous, I found interacting with our customers very satisfying. We saw the same folks on a regular basis, knew them by name, and knew some of the most intimate details of their life by virtue of filling their prescriptions.

It's sad to say that we were often the last line of defense for a patient prescribed medicines by different physicians who didn't pay attention to what the other was using to treat a different condition.

Until early 1996, drug interactions where about the most dramatic thing we encountered. Then the FDA approved a new narcotic for the treatment of pain, oxycodone hydrochloride, which was sold under the name OxyContin. The manufacturer had their drug reps, mostly good-looking, college-educated up and comers, pushing the drug to physicians. The marketing hype claimed there was a low possibility of it being addictive.

Physicians and their families attended exclusive conferences in desirable destinations like Las Vegas, Orlando, and Hawaii, all courtesy of the manufacturer. The physicians only had to sit through a one-hour presentation for a week's free vacation.

OxyContin, known on the street as Oxy, was soon flying off pharmacy shelves. Pain management clinics were opening all over the country. The more prescriptions for OxyContin a physician wrote the more kickbacks they received.

More drug reps were hired and encouraged to push oxycodone. The only difference between the drug reps and the drug pushers on the street corners was the drug reps were legal. Both were pushing addictive drugs. Everyone was making money hand over fist. In 1996 sales of the drug by the manufacturer were $48 million and by 2000 sales had climbed to $1.1 billion. They were part of one of the biggest drug rings ever in the United States and it was all legal.

There was only one problem, Oxy was highly addictive. In one small town in Kentucky a pharmacy sold enough Oxy in one year to give every person in the town over 2,000 pills.

In our local Walgreens, we saw a rising number of prescriptions from local pain management doctors come through the pharmacy. We also had access to data on the total number of prescriptions for Oxy from all providers. It was clear a serious problem was brewing, and I raised my concern with my managers. Nothing prepared us for the magnitude of the crisis.

Florida didn't have a system to monitor drug prescriptions so people would travel from one clinic to another buying hundreds of doses of prescription drugs in one day. Florida soon had the highest number of prescriptions for Oxy in the country and was known by users as the Florida Express. When I drove by these pill mills, license plates were from all over the Southeast. There was an opioid crisis in the nation that was killing people every day and destroying families, but little was being done about it.

Eventually, cases were brought against physicians for unlawfully prescribing opioids. Across the United States from California to the hills of East Tennessee, Michigan, Vermont, and Florida, arrests were made, and doctors were sent to prison.

The head of the opioid snake was Purdue Pharma, and it was also being prosecuted. In 2019 Purdue pled guilty in federal court in Newark, New Jersey to conspiracy to defraud the United States and violate the anti-kickback statute.

Company executives admitted that it marketed and sold its dangerous opioid products to healthcare providers even though it had reason to believe those providers were diverting them to abusers. The company lied to the DEA about steps it had taken to prevent such diversion, fraudulently increasing the amount of its products it was permitted to sell.

Purdue also admitted it paid kickbacks to providers to encourage them to prescribe even more of its products. The company was ordered to pay a criminal fine of $3.544 billion dollars and a criminal forfeiture of $2 billion dollars. The Sackler family, who owned Purdue Pharma, agreed to pay $225 million in damages and the company filed for bankruptcy.

In part of the settlement, the Sackler family sought protection from other lawsuits, which a lower court ruled against. After years of further litigation, a United States appeals court ordered a $6 billion opioid settlement, but reversed the prior lower court decision. Now the family could shield themselves from opioid-related lawsuits despite not filing for bankruptcy. The case was appealed to the Supreme Court to overturn the protections for the Sackler family and in 2023 the Supreme Court agreed, the protections should be dropped. All the litigation was civil, neither the Sacklers, nor any Purdue executives, were criminally charged.

Meanwhile, the states began legal action against national pharmacy chains, charging they contributed to the opioid crisis by not monitoring abnormal prescribing patterns for Oxy. In my state of Florida, my employer, Walgreens, agreed to pay $620 million, and CVS agreed to pay $440 million.

It was a long-awaited partial win for the good guys, which came too late for the thousands of people who died from opioid addiction and their families. However, in the court of public opinion, museums, universities, and other institutions around the world, who had received Sackler family donations and endowments, stripped the Sackler name from buildings and programs.

CHAPTER 26

In March 1996 JB called. He and Selma were flying down to Lakeland during spring break so the twins could visit Florida Southern College.

"Senior prom is in April and graduation in early May and then the summer ski tournaments. Julia wants to go to Florida Southern on a water ski scholarship and study nursing."

"It's a great school, she'll be very happy there and it will be wonderful having her close by," I said, "What about Jane?"

"The FSC ski coach has been scouting the girls since they were in the ninth grade, and after their junior year, she offered them scholarships. Julia signed, but Jane has her heart set on following in her mom's footsteps and wants to pursue her degree at Embry Riddle and become a commercial pilot. We're going to visit both schools on this trip."

"I can't believe the twins are ready for college," I said.

"Neither can we. Seems like yesterday we were changing diapers. Speaking of diapers, how's Elisabeth Anne? Have you spoiled her to the max, yet. You know that's a grandparent's priority, spoil the kid and give her back to the parents."

"Thanks for asking. She's beautiful and we are excelling at our responsibilities as grandparents, nothing's too good for that one."

"Between flying and going to ski tournaments the summer will be over before we know it so I hope we can get together when we're in Lakeland."

"Of course, we'll make it happen, give us a call when you get in."

"Will do. We'll see you guys soon."

The twins who had grown into beautiful young women. Water skiing had toned their bodies and the sun had tanned their skin. JB had a full-time job keeping the young men of Wachataw county at bay. By the time they were seniors in high school, the girls were rated in the top ten of skiers in the country. Their trophies and ribbons filled their rooms and just about every bit of shelf space in the house.

On June 6, 2002, I got a call from my old friend George. He could barely speak.

"Right, Sashiko died this morning, the cancer finally took her. PK and I are going to take her ashes back to Wakkanai for the funeral and burial in her family plot. We'd like for you and Sue to go with us. JB and Selma are coming, but I especially want you and Sue to come because you were there when Sashiko and I got married and we spent good times together in Japan. I need you and Sue to be with me."

"George, I have no words. I'm so sorry for your loss, for our loss. Sashiko is in a better place, and she doesn't have to suffer any longer. You know Sue and I will be there with you. Give PK our love."

It was a sad reunion of the three musketeers for Sahiko's funeral at the Hokumon Shinto Shrine overlooking Wakkanai. George followed the centuries-old traditions of a Japanese funeral, assisted by PK, who was in dress uniform bearing the Army Air Assault and Aviator badges.

JB, Selma, Sue, and I stopped in Misawa on the way back to Tokyo. They say you can't go home, and it was true about our visit to Misawa. Like us, much had changed in the 33 years since we had caught the Air America flight in 1969 for our trip back to Alabama.

Less than a year later, on March 20th, our hearts were broken again when George called to tell us PK had been killed in Iraq. Our conversation was short, and I knew George Daniel was hanging on by a thread. I called JB, "He's out of his mind with grief. He's in a bad way. I'm worried."

Sue and I immediately got a flight out of Tampa to D.C. where we met JB and Selma. At George's townhouse, we found him curled up on the floor in a catatonic state. Sue called 911 and he was admitted to Walter Reed Hospital's psychiatric unit. PK was not buried in Arlington Cemetery until April 21st when George was discharged from the hospital to attend the funeral.

Before Sue and I returned to Florida George promised me he would go to grief counseling. When we got home, I called to check in on him, but he didn't answer the phone. I called JB and shared my concern, but JB felt we had to let George grieve in his own way. JB had experience with trauma and grief, so I respected his opinion. "He'll be in touch when he's ready. I know where he is, and I know he's okay."

George didn't keep his promise and I didn't hear from him for years. On June 3, 2020, JB called to tell me that George had been injured during a demonstration in Lafayette Park in Washington D.C. He was hospitalized and unconscious. George had a comfortable home and was financially secure, but since the loss of Sashiko and PK his home and his heart were empty. George had been living in the park and he poured his grief into protest holding the government, which he had so admirably served, accountable. He was a fixture in the activist community, known as Doomsday Dan, and he was respected and liked by the homeless and politicians alike.

George recovered from his injuries and fell in love again. On December 12, 2022, he married Millie Jacobs, the nurse who had cared for him during his rehabilitation. During his time in Lafayette Park, George enjoyed a regular game of dominoes with a powerful Senator. They engaged in robust conversations about politics, power and greed, and a friendship developed. George's old dominoes buddy was now the President of the United States. Not long after Millie and George returned to D.C. from their honeymoon, the President called to offer George the Ambassadorship to Japan. Although honored to be considered, George politely declined the President's offer. Japan held too many memories.

In January, when the Ambassador to Greece was killed in a car accident the President called again and asked George to take the job. The ultra-conservative and conspiracy nuts thought it comical the President has nominated a street person to be the Ambassador to Greece. Under the U.S. Constitution, with the advice and consent of the Senate, the President may nominate ambassadors. Republican senators vigorously objected, claiming that George wasn't qualified for the position. During the nomination process the public learned of George's military service, his master's degree from Georgetown, and his International Law degree. He was more qualified than any Ambassador nominated by the prior two administrations, and he was approved by the Democratic majority.

In June 2023, Sue and I visited George and Millie in Athens. We were getting old and if we didn't make the trip soon, we might never get to visit Greece. Sue had Greece on her bucket list after watching My Big Fat Greek Wedding and I wanted to visit Meteora that was featured in the James Bond film, "For His Eyes Only".

I tried to contact *International Travel* magazine to see if they would be interested in paying us for an article about our trip to Greece, but the phone number was no longer in service. Were they, like many magazines, victims of the digital age, or did the CIA just move on to other ways of conducting their covert activities? After our brief conversation about the cocaine bust, I never heard from Gill again.

CHAPTER 28

On September 8th, Sue's eightieth birthday, we boarded the Delta flight to Atlanta to connect with the 5 PM flight to Athens. We splurged on business-class seats which were life savers on the ten-and-a-half-hour flight from Atlanta to Athens. I slept on a plane for the first time. Sue, who also could never sleep on a plane, was snoring softly after two glasses of champagne and the best dinner we ever had on a commercial flight.

We were met at the airport by Ambassador and Mrs. Franklin, escorted by their Diplomatic Security Services bodyguards, and driven in a bulletproof black SUV to the apartment Millie had rented for us located a half mile from the American Embassy and a twenty-minute walk to Syntagma Square. Millie had stocked the kitchen with food, coffee, and Greek wine. George apologized for not being able to stay and show us the city, but he had a meeting with the Greek president.

After unpacking our bags and freshening up, we were ready for a tour of Athens. Record heat and summer wildfires were in the past and the cooler September temperatures with fewer tourists were a welcome surprise. With diplomatic car tags, our driver didn't have to circle for a parking space. Our first stop was a small taverna in the neighborhood. After the best lamb souvlaki, I had ever eaten, it was off to the tomb of the Unknown Soldier to watch the changing of the guard.

The crowd grew as it came time for the ceremony. It felt strange to have bodyguards following us, but they ensured a tight perimeter around Millie. As the new detail guarding the tomb made their entrance, their colorful, unique uniforms immediately drew my attention. Each guard wore a scarlet fez, a shirt with wide sleeves, a pleated kilt, waistcoat, and red leather clogs with black pompoms. Their high-kicking march delighted the crowd. Sue recorded the entire ceremony and posted it on Facebook. Just as the ceremony ended, our SUV pulled up and we were whisked away to our next stop, the Dionysus Theater entrance to the Acropolis.

I noticed a rather lengthy line to purchase tickets at the Acropolis, but Millie flashed her diplomatic credentials, and we entered as guests of the Greek government. Just inside, a group of tour guides waited to offer their services. I engaged a young lady, Eleni Papadopoulos, who spoke particularly good English. She was a college student majoring in Greek history. As we traversed pathways of uneven stones, worn smooth by thousands of feet over the centuries, I was thankful we wore our good walking shoes.

Eleni told us the Dionysus Theater dates to 600 BC and was named for the god of wine. It had a capacity of 25,000 and in its day was used for plays and government meetings. As we stood looking down on the outdoor amphitheater, I imagined the noise of 25,000 Greeks enjoying a Greek tragedy play before the time of Christ. Eleni took my phone and snapped a picture of Sue and me with the theater in the background.

As we walked further in the Acropolis, we came to the Odeon Herodes Atticus Theater, another open-air amphitheater which Eleni explained was built in 161 AD by Herodes Atticus in memory of his Roman wife, Aspasia Annia Regilla. It originally was a steep-sloped theater with a three-story stone front wall and a wooden roof made of cedar of Lebanon timber. Used as a music venue, with a capacity of 5,000, it was destroyed and left in ruins in 267 AD. Restored and re-opened in 1955 it is the main venue for the Athens Festival from May through October each year. Frank Sinatra, Maria Callas, Elton John, and many other prominent artists have performed at the Odeon. Woody Allen and his New Orleans Jazz band was scheduled to perform that evening.

After more pictures, we continued our walk towards the Parthenon. We learned that the Parthenon was built between 447 and 432 BC during the height of the ancient Greek Empire. It was dedicated in 438 BC to the Greek goddess Athena. In the 6th century AD Christian Byzantines conquered Greece and outlawed pagan worship and converted the Parthenon to a Christian Church. It remained a Christian Church until 1458 AD when the Muslim Ottoman Empire seized Athens and converted it to a mosque.

Greece remained under Turkish control for almost 400 years. During the war for Greek independence from 1821 to 1832, the Acropolis became a war zone and the Turkish army removed hundreds of marble blocks from the Parthenon and used the lead coated clamps that held the blocks together to make bullets. The Parthenon lay in ruins and was subject to the ravages of looters and the elements. In the early 19th century, the Seventh Earl of Elgin stole the marble friezes and several marble statues and took them to England where they are on display in the British Museum. England has refused to return them.

I mentioned to Eleni that we wanted to see Meteora and asked if she could recommend a tour company. Coincidentally, she was leading a tour to Meteora the next morning and invited the three of us to join her. Millie declined as she had other obligations but encouraged us to go.

Our tour for the day was complete and Eleni led us down from the Acropolis to the gate that led to the Platka, the shopping area. We agreed to meet at the train station the next morning at 7 for a 7:20 departure. Millie had one more stop she wanted us to make, the Aphrodite Gold and Silver Jewelry shop.

"Aphrodite's has been the official jewelry store for Americans since 1977 and is popular with embassy staff. Georgios Nikolopoulos, the owner of the shop, served the Americans when there was an Air Force base in Athens. His jewelry has adorned the necks of wives and girlfriends of military men, and famous USO performers for over 45 years," Millie explained.

I didn't expect the friendly greeting we received when we walked into the shop. Georgios addressed Millie by name and kissed her and Sue on their cheeks. When Millie introduced me, he wrapped his arms around me and kissed me on both cheeks. Sue explained that she was interested in buying a gold cartouche with her name engraved on it. She ended up buying five more as Christmas presents personalized for Stephanie, Elisabeth Anne, Selma, and the twins.

Our old legs had walked about as far as we could for one day, so Millie called for the car to pick us up and drop us off at the apartment. We walked to the nearby neighborhood taverna and enjoyed a light supper.

Bright and early Sunday morning we met Eleni on platform 8. We were extra cautious having been warned that the train station was notorious for pickpockets. Our train arrived right on time and our group was directed to reserved seats in car number five. The four-hour ride to Kalambaka, the city where we would catch the tour bus to Meteora, carried us over hills and mountains, through tunnels, across exceedingly high trestles over deep gorges, and through coastal plains. The scenery was breathtaking. To my surprise, we passed cotton fields as big as the ones in the Delta of Mississippi. Eleni informed us that Greece is the largest producer of cotton in Europe, over 1.3 million bales.

As we traveled through the hills, she pointed out peach orchards and informed the group that Greece is the third largest producer of peaches in the world behind China and Italy. When I think of agriculture in Greece, I think of olives and grapes, not cotton and peaches. We were seeing parts of Greece that most tourists never see, far from Athens and the islands everyone imagines when they think of Greece.

When the train pulled into the Kalambaka station we were met by an air-conditioned van and began our tour. The large rock formations and the monasteries at the summit were breathtaking. A total of 24 monasteries were built and six are still active. Our first stop was the Monastery of Holy Trinity which was famous for being featured in "For His Eyes Only". Built before the 14th century, it's the oldest and largest of the monasteries sitting on top of a rock 400 feet in the air. We descended a path to the base of the rock where 145 carved steps lead up to the visitors center. After stopping to rest three times, we finally made it to the top. The magnificent views were worth the labor of the climb. I was more impressed with the views than I was with the monastery and only had to rest once going down.

The rest of the afternoon was spent visiting three more monasteries. By the time we got back to the train station, we were two very weary travelers. We had just enough time to grab pitas to eat on the train ride back to Athens. After our meal, the clicky-clack of the train soon put us to sleep. Stopping at the Athens station woke us up and we caught a cab back to the apartment and fell into bed just before midnight.

After two active days we looked forward to sleeping late and resting up, but Millie had other plans. "Pack an overnight bag, we are going to the Peloponnese. George has been promising to take me but work always gets in the way. I made reservations for us in a renovated 17th century mansion in Nafplio."

We packed our bags, grabbed a quick bite to eat and we were off. After leaving the intercity traffic we drove the Greek National Highway toward the Peloponnese. Our first stop was the Corinth Canal. The ancient Greeks first attempted to dig a canal more than two thousand years ago, but it wasn't completed until 1893. Its sheer rock walls are a testament to the enormous engineering accomplishment. We were traveling in the footsteps of Paul the Apostle. We soon came to the site of the church where Paul preached to the Corinthians. Nothing was left but rocks, but when I closed my eyes, I was transported back in time and could hear Paul's words.

Our next stop was Acrocorinth, a hilltop fortress considered one of the finest in Greece built thousands of years ago. We continued along the National Highway with the beautiful blue waters of the Aegean Sea off to our right. Our next stop was the ancient Olympiad which sits in the shadows of Mount Kconos. I walked along the track of the stadium where nearly 3,000 years before the first Olympic games were held as a tribute to the god Zeus. The sun above and the rumbling in our stomachs told us it was time to eat lunch. After lunch, we traveled to Epidaurus, the site of a 14,000-seat theater built in the fourth century BCE. To my amazement it is almost perfectly intact. It is used today and has almost perfect acoustics.

We turned back towards Athens and arrived in Nafplio as the sun was setting. Nafplio is a port city with a 400-year-old Palamidi fortress which had guarded the city for centuries. Nafplio was the first capital of Greece after the Greeks won their independence from Turkey. Our hotel was a renovated 17th century mansion with views of the ocean. After a late dinner we walked through the old city and along the seashore. The lights illuminating Palamidi gave the city a fairy tale ambiance.

Tuesday morning, we enjoyed brunch and drove back to Athens. Before going to the apartment, we stopped at Aphrodite Jewelry Shop to pick up the six gold cartouches that Sue had ordered.

CHAPTER 29

Another item on my bucket list was to take a cruise on a sailing yacht in the Greek Islands. Before we left the States, Sue and I charted *Dream On*, an Atlantic 55 Catamaran out of the Agio Kosmas Sailing Center. The yacht boasting four passenger cabins and a crew cabin was owned by a retired USAF Lieutenant Colonel, Bill Withers, and his Greek wife, Maria. They had no crew, Bill captains the boat and Maria is the first mate, chief cook, and deck hand.

Bill and Maria live on *Dream On* full time and each December they sail across the Atlantic to St. Thomas in the U.S. Virgin Islands and return to Greece in late May. Both Millie and George were supposed to join us, but George got tied up with official business and had to beg off.

After a safety briefing by Captain Withers, we left the harbor at 4:30 in the afternoon. As we sailed into the Saronic Gulf, Bill asked if I would like to take the helm. He dialed in the GPS coordinates for the Island of Aegina which was the first stop on our trip. We had a good wind which kept the mainsail full without having to tack back and forth. I had sailed small boats on the lake at home, but this was my first time sailing a large yacht. After the sun set we enjoyed a delicious meal and local Greek wine under a sky filled with more stars than I had ever seen. As *Dream On* sailed towards our first destination, I felt a deep peace. The only sounds were quiet conversations of the people on deck, the water splashing against the bow of the boat, and the hum of the wind flowing through the sail. After six hours of smooth sailing, we saw the lights on the island of Aegina. I turned the wheel over to the captain and helped Maria with the lines as Bill expertly eased the boat up to the dock.

It was 10:30, my normal bedtime back in Florida, but in Greece people were still sitting in the outdoor cafes eating dinner and drinking wine. The three of us joined Bill and Maria at their favorite cafe for dessert and coffee and I finally climbed into bed after midnight.

The smell of freshly brewed coffee and the sound of angry seagulls woke me from a deep sleep at 8:30. Bill and Maria had breakfast ready on deck. We had three hours free to explore the village and visit the Temple of Aegina. Maria recommended a cafe where we could get a light lunch. After taking way too many pictures, we made it back to the dock in time for departure for the island of Poros.

The wind that day was stronger, so Bill took the wheel. Conditions required that he tack back and forth to keep us on course, but we made good time, and we docked as the sun was setting next to a yacht flying the Australian flag. *Stayin' Alive* looked to be about 150 feet long. Sue and I stood admiring her when a couple appeared from the cabin. They waved and the man called out to us in an Australian accent, "Hey mates, would you like to come aboard for a cocktail?"

Sue and I looked at each, knowing what the other was thinking *We have to see that yacht!* "Yes, we would, thanks for the invite."

We cautiously made it down one gangway and up another to the deck of *Stayin' Alive*.

"Welcome aboard, I'm Alex McKlentoc and this is my wife, Shirley." Alex had a radiant smile, a strong handshake, and a golden tan.

"Glad to meet you. I'm Robert Talbert, and this is my wife, Sue."

"Everyone calls him Right Hand," Sue offered, "Thank you for having us aboard."

As our hosts led us to a sitting area at the stern, Alex's brow furrowed as if trying to remember something, "You wouldn't be from Alabama by any chance?" he asked.

Glancing at Sue in surprise, I answered, "Yes, I was originally from Alabama, but we live in Florida now."

"Were you, or are you, a pharmacist?" was his next question.

Strains of that alternative universe I experienced when meeting Gill Maxwell reverberated through my body. Wondering what I had gotten us into by accepting this invitation, I said, "This is getting strange, how do you know this?"

Alex chuckled, "Well, I could tell from your Southern drawl that you must be from the Southern U.S. and my father had a favorite story he told about a pharmacist, named Right Hand from Alabama, who went on two Open Doors missions to China with him. He got a kick out of your nickname because Dad was also left-handed and laughed when he talked about his friend Right Hand."

I was dumbfounded. "Damn, it's a small world, are you Shawn McKlentoc's son?"

"One and only. Come on, let's sit and enjoy the evening and a glass of wine."

"How is your father?" I asked as we got comfortable.

"Oh, Dad passed away in 2017, just after he sold the family business. I stayed on as CEO until June of this year when I decided that there must be more to life than just work. This boat belonged to a Russian billionaire who fell out of a window. Lots of that going around lately. It's been tied up in Istanbul since last year and I bought it at a bargain price. We had a renaming ceremony to appease the gods and ward of the bad luck, and here we are."

Shirley offered Sue a tour and they excused themselves. The chatter of voices coming from below drifted to our aft deck.

"That's our three rugrats doing their homework. We're on a world cruise. We locked up the house, hired a nurse and a tutor for the girls and set sail."

Our drinks were served by a young man in a white uniform who looked like he might be from the Philippines.

"How many crew do you have?" I asked.

"We run with a crew of nine plus the tutor and nurse. We have six state rooms plus the crew cabins."

We enjoyed a bottle of wine over good conversation and by the time Alex gave me the captain's tour my stomach was rumbling. "Alex, Shirley, it was a real pleasure meeting you both. If you get to Florida during your tour, give us a call," I said.

"We'll be spending the winter in Portugal, then sailing to England and the Nordic countries next spring and summer. After that we'll be sailing to Canada and the U.S. Maybe we can meet you then."

We exchanged contacts and Sue and I disembarked and walked to shore. "What kind of business did Alex's father own?" she asked.

"Shawn was an interesting character. He owned the largest TV network in Australia and a movie studio, and he was a billionaire, but he told everyone he was a sheep farmer. He was raised on the largest sheep station in Australia, over one million-hectares. His family is the largest producer of wool in the country and owns eight sheep stations. He was a humble man of great faith and the Open Doors missions to China would not have been possible without his financial backing."

When we woke the next morning, *Stayin' Alive* was gone. We spent the day exploring the island of Poros, which sits in the center of the Saronic Gulf, wandering through town admiring the beautiful neoclassical buildings from past eras. Friday night we gathered at the Poseidon Taverna for dinner. The wine and food were exceptional.

Early Saturday morning we set sail for the island of Hydra. Several other yachts were sailing in the same direction. Just after lunch, the seas grew rough with a heavy wind coming out of the north. Bill explained that the winds are called Meltemi and are common from June through August, but that they can also last into September. They are caused by high-pressure over the Balkans and low-pressure over Turkey. The wind became so strong Bill had to strike the sail and start the motor. As we motored towards Hydra, the boat was bucking like a bronco.

We pulled into the harbor, and I understood why people say Hydra is the most beautiful port in Greece. The rough seas and high winds were causing boats to seek out a safe harbor to wait out the winds and there was only one berth open where Bill could dock the boat. We secured the lines and decided to go ashore to explore. Sue and Millie went below deck to put on their walking shoes while I waited on deck. I watched as another yacht entered the harbor and backed up to our boat. The name emblazoned in gold lettering on her stern was *Romanoff*. A deck hand threw me a line and I tied it to a cleat on our boat.

An imposing middle-aged man emerged from the cabin, walked across the deck of the yacht, and stepped over onto our boat. I welcomed him aboard, but he didn't respond. He untied the line from the cleat that I had just secured, walked the length of our boat, and tied the line to a cleat on the dock. As if he owned the place, he walked back to his boat, placed the line in a winch and began winching his boat into the small space between our boat and the yacht next to us.

It was obvious there was not enough room to dock *Romanoff*, so I shouted to him to stop winching. He replied, "No speak English" and continued to winch. His boat began rubbing against the bumpers on our boat and the yacht on the opposite side. A man on that boat also yelled to stop winching. He got the same reply, "No speak English".

"No speak English" started yelling at our neighbor who responded in a language that I didn't understand. Suddenly, our neighbor reached into his pocket, pulled out a hawk-billed sailor's knife and opened the blade. He yelled something at the interloper on *Romanoff* and we watched in disbelief as the man winched another turn. In a swift motion, our neighbor reached out and cut the asshole's line which precipitated more yelling. The uninvited guest also pulled out a knife reached down and cut the line to my neighbor's Zodiac dinghy, which drifted off into the harbor. There was more yelling as the newcomer jumped down on our boat and tied the line to a cleat. Everyone around us had heard the yelling and we all watched, stunned, as this guy walked across the deck to the wharf and off towards the town.

"Can you believe the nerve of that Russian asshole?" our neighbor remarked.

"What a rude son-of-a-bitch," I concurred, "That was Russian you were speaking?"

"Yes, and that's the attitude you get from the oligarchs. He claims to be an architect and able to estimate distance better than anyone else."

"I don't care what he is, there's no way his boat was going to fit into that space without doing damage to our boats," said Bill, who had come on deck when he heard the commotion.

"I told him if he winched the line one more time I would cut his line, he did, so I did," pausing, our neighbor said, "I'm sorry, I should have introduced myself, I'm James O'Brien."

"Bill Withers. This is my wife Maria, and our guests Robert and Sue Talbert, and Millie Franklin."

Movement along the wharf caught my eye and I squinted into the sun. The rude Russian was hurrying toward our boat followed by a policeman who was struggling to keep up. When they got to our boat the policeman said something in Greek. James responded to him in Greek and then turned to Bill and me.

"You're not going to believe this, but he's here to arrest us for denying this asshole access to the shore. He says we have to go with him to the police station."

James turned to Bill, "My girlfriend, Alexia, should be back in a short while. She's a lawyer for the largest maritime law firm in Athens. Tell her to come to the police station."

Millie looked on in shock. I hugged Sue and told her not to worry, it was all a misunderstanding and joined James and the policeman for our perp walk down the dock. When we arrived at the station we were fingerprinted, our mugshots taken, and we were placed into one of the two jail cells. The other cell was occupied by a man who seemed to be sleeping off a drunk. There was a bench along the wall and a dirty commode in the corner. We sat down to await the arrival of Alexia.

Finally, an hour after we were locked up, Alexia and her cousin showed up and we were given a time for our hearing and released.

Back at the boat, Millie called George and told him about our arrest. He asked her to put Alexia on the phone and after a short conversation, Alexia assured him that she would clear up the misunderstanding.

Greeks eat late and they hold court late as well. We arrived a few minutes before 10 PM for our hearing and waited in the courtroom for the judge. Alexia introduced herself to the judge and told him which firm she worked for and said she was representing James and me. The judge requested the police report, read it, and asked how we pled to the charge of denying the Russian access to the shore. Alexia answered not guilty on our behalf. I couldn't understand a word that was spoken. In hindsight it was comical; Alexia translated each word from Greek to English for me and James translated everything into Russian for the rude asshole who didn't speak Greek very well.

When asked, I presented my version of events of when *Romanoff* entered the harbor and offered a picture on my phone of the Russian's boat tied to Bill's. The judge looked closely at the photograph and returned my phone to Alexia. With nothing further said or done, the judge ruled that we had handled the situation appropriately by the law and apologized for the arrest. He reprimanded the policeman for a shoddy investigation, because as my picture clearly showed, *Romanoff* was tethered to *Dream On* and there was unimpeded access to the shore.

By this time, the Russian was fuming. The judge asked him how many meters of line he had lost and ordered James to pay for four meters. He then asked James the value of the Zodiac the Russian had cut loose. James said he had paid 24,000 Euros for the boat in 2020 just before the pandemic. The judge told the Russian that his boat would be impounded and could not leave the harbor until he paid James the cost of the Zodiac, or it was found undamaged and returned to James.

The judge had more to say. He ruled that the Russian had no right of access to *Dream On*'s deck to get to his boat. The Russian couldn't contain himself any longer, and according to James' translation, he asked the judge how he was supposed to get back on his boat. James translated the judge's answer for the Russian, "Take a water taxi or swim. I don't give a damn how you get back."

James paid twelve Euros for the line which the court recorded. The judge then pounded his gavel and said the case was dismissed. The Russian followed us back to our boats and began to come aboard *Dream On* when James blocked his way and told him in Russian where he could hire a water taxi.

We awoke the next morning to find the line to the Russian's boat cut and the *Romanoff* gone. The Zodiac was tied to a cleat. After the excitement of the previous evening, we spent the next day exploring the island, shopping, and swimming in the crystal-clear water. In the late afternoon, we walked out to a bar on the rocks overlooking the Aegean and watched the sun set into the ocean. It was one of the most beautiful sunsets I've ever seen.

Monday morning, we said goodbye to Hydra and motored back to Athens. We arrived as the sun was setting and the lights in the harbor were coming on. We thanked Bill and Maria for an exciting and enjoyable cruise, and they invited us to visit them in St. Thomas for Christmas.

Tuesday, we visited the National Museum and packed up for our flight back to the States. That evening we enjoyed one last dinner with Millie and George at a taverna in the Platka.

Our flight home was uneventful, and it felt good to sleep in our own beds. Thursday morning, I woke early and decided to go for a walk. As I walked up the hill from the lake I felt a pain in my chest, and everything went black.

I was back in 1966 and dancing with Sue at the Maxwell Air Force Base Officers Club. Our favorite slow song was playing on the jukebox.

Goodnight sweetheart, well it's time to go,

Goodnight sweetheart, well it's time to go,

I hate to leave you, but I really must say,

Oh, goodnight sweetheart, goodnight.

I felt Sue kissing me goodbye.

The song ended and all was quiet.

EPILOGUE

A maintenance man cutting grass saw me fall and called 911. Stephanie and Sue were among curious neighbors who followed the EMTs down the road to the lake. I had regained consciousness, but it felt like an elephant had sat on my chest and I was having a tough time breathing.

Sue was beside herself as the ambulance took me away. HAT, Sue, and Stephanie followed it to the hospital and the next morning I had triple bypass surgery. Due to the wonders of modern medicine, three days later I was discharged from the hospital. A week later I going to cardiac rehab three times a week.

At a check-up one month after they cracked my chest and performed the triple bypass, my cardiologist told me I was an incredibly lucky man. My prognosis was good, but he stressed the need for regular exercise and suggested daily walking.

Elisabeth Anne never played baseball, but she excelled at soccer and went to college on a full scholarship. She is in her last year of residency in orthopedic surgery.

HAT retired from the major leagues and is the head baseball coach at Florida Southern College. JB and Selma sold their crop-dusting service and moved to Lakeland. We get together once a week to go out to dinner. Their daughter Julia is a nurse practitioner in Orlando and her sister Jane is a pilot with Delta Airlines.

George and Millie bought the last lot on the lake in our subdivision and are building a house where they intend to live when George finishes his term as Ambassador to Greece in 2024.

Sue plays bridge every week and one of the ladies in her group fosters dogs for the local shelter. Every now and then she brings one to the bridge game to aid in socializing the dog to give it a better chance at adoption. One week she showed up with a 6-month-old, full-bred miniature Schnauzer by the name of Maggie.

There is something special about Maggie who has a bed in our living room and another in our bedroom.

We walk every morning and most afternoons. The neighbors stop to say hello and to pet Maggie, who is always looking for affection and someone to rub her head.

She's known by everyone. Me? I'm no longer Right Hand, I'm that old man who walks Maggie.

AUTHOR BIO

Colonel James Gallman is a retired Medical Service Corp officer, who worked in hospitals all over the world, both as a military member and as a civilian. He and his wife Pat reside in Lakeland, Florida and have two sons, Jay, and John.

During the Covid-19 pandemic he embarked on a bucket-list item and began writing. While walking Maggie one day, he introduced himself to a new neighbor which led to the publication of his three books in the Farkenfield Trilogy.

A history buff and fan of historical fiction, Jim is currently working on his fourth book and is immersed in research on the USS Alabama and long-haul truckers.